Second in the violent
brutal American West .

Claw 2

VENGEANCE ROAD

By the same author

Day of Fury

MATTHEW KIRK

Vengeance Road

GRANADA
London Toronto Sydney New York

Published by Granada Publishing Limited in 1983

ISBN 0 583 13555 2

A Granada Paperback Original

Granada Publishing Limited
Frogmore, St Albans, Herts AL2 2NF
and
36 Golden Square, London W1R 4AH
515 Madison Avenue, New York, NY 10022, USA
117 York Street, Sydney, NSW 2000, Australia
100 Skyway Avenue, Rexdale, Ontario, M9W 3A6, Canada
61 Beach Road, Auckland, New Zealand

Printed and bound in Great Britain by
Cox and Wyman Ltd, Reading
Set in Times

The blacktop is lonely now: there is an empty space which will not be filled. This book is dedicated to the memory of Warren Oates, 1932–1982.

Chapter One

The man sat in shadow, immobile. There were birds in the big pine that both hid him and sheltered him from the hot Mexican sun, but they ignored the silent shape sprawled on the ground below. The man was equally incurious, his cold grey eyes fastened on the entrance to the shallow bowl spread before him. He was on a ridge, the higher ground circling protectively against the flank of the mountains that jutted bare-boned against the sky. Within the confines of the curving ridge the ground was richly grassed, a spring pooling blue water behind a stand of cottonwoods. Beyond the water and the trees there was the ruin of a hacienda, the roof caved in, the windows staring blank and dead into the sunlight. A monotonous buzzing came from the ruin, as though a horde of flies feasted behind the adobe walls. Two horses cropped grass in a makeshift corral on the farther side of the building, tails twitching in the heat. The entrance to the bowl was a narrow split in the ridge, clearly visible from the man's position, approached along a steep trail winding up through the Sonoran highlands.

The grey eyes that watched the entrance were as remorseless as the blinding silver-gold disc of the sun. There was hate in them, and grief; mostly a hard, cold anger that seemed coalesced in a gaze of fixed determination. The face was lean, tanned, beard stubble darkening a powerful jaw. Thick, dark brown hair framed the features, falling over the collar of a dirty white shirt. He wore black pants, the cuffs hanging over scuffed, well-worn boots of the same colour. One knee was raised, supporting a black stetson. Around his waist there was a black leather gunbelt, the cutaway holster containing a

Colt's Peacemaker in .45 calibre, the fingers of his right hand spread lightly on the wood grips.

He had no left hand.

Where there should have been flesh, there was metal. Where skin should have covered bone and veins and tendons there was instead a gleaming steel fist, rounded smoothly, tapering to the end, where three blades protruded. The blades were each about four inches long, curving claw-like to needle points, the undersides honed to razor sharpness. The appendage was fastened over the stump of his wrist by a harness of leather straps. It looked deadly.

The man's name was Tyler Wyatt.

Once he had been a blacksmith.

Once he had had a wife.

Once he had had two hands.

Now he hunted the men who had taken those things from him.

He had caught up with two of them. They were inside the hacienda: a banquet for the flies and the scavenging creatures he had heard in the night. His mouth stretched in an ugly smile as he thought of them. Wade Martin and Andy Chance. They had paid for that day back in Black Rock. Paid for what they did to Josie. To him. And now they would bring him the Creole, Jean DuPré; like rotting meat in a hunter's lure.

And DuPré would lead him to Vance Jennings. To Simon Coltrane. To the scarred mute, Strother Cannon.

He murmured the names: a litany of hate.

He had been waiting for two days now. Two long days since the claws had torn answers from the killers. A lifetime from Black Rock. But he could wait longer: the anger would still be there; and with it, patience. The patience of the hunter who can see no other outcome than the kill. The trail was already old, but he could still follow it. Would, for he had no other purpose: there was nothing else.

Chance had told him of their plan. Down the mountain the Villalta mine was readying a shipment of silver for transport to the border. Vance Jennings would be waiting there, with Coltrane and Strother Cannon. Chance and Martin were back-up, waiting for DuPré to bring them word. But DuPré would find only their corpses, and that should send him running back to Jennings. Back with Wyatt on his tail.

The lean-faced man smiled as he thought about it. It made the waiting easier.

'I don't like it.' Jean DuPré stroked the smooth curves of his black moustache, his handsome face creased in a frown. 'I am sorry, Vance, but it smells bad to me.'

'The hell it does!' Jennings' voice was a harsh whisper, as though the words strained his vocal cords. He fingered the bandanna wound high around his neck, scratching at the scar that stretched whitely across his throat. 'We go ahead. Just like I said.'

'With Rafe killed?' DuPré drank tequila. Took salt and lemon from the bowl between them. 'Butchered like that?'

Jennings shrugged and pushed black hair that was streaked with grey from his seamed brown face. 'Rafe was a lawman on the make. He crossed people. Anyone coulda killed him. Indians, maybe.'

'Like that?' the Creole repeated. 'He was hacked apart.'

'Indians work that way.' Jennings turned, twisting his shoulders as though his neck had lost its full mobility to stare at Strother Cannon. 'Like they did on Strother.'

The Creole followed his gaze. Strother Cannon stared back, mouth spread in a broad smile. Sweat glistened on his bald skull, droplets gathering in the puckered scar tissue where the hairline should have started. Across his face there lay a tracery of scars, one eye tugged down by the same line that curled his lip in a permanent sneer. His nostrils flared back from a nose without a tip, the poorly healed flesh an angry red against the darkness of his skin. DuPré turned to face Jennings again.

'Perhaps,' he acknowledged. 'Perhaps not.'

'Maybe Jean's turnin' yellow.' Simon Coltrane was insignificant beside the tortured ugliness of Cannon, a slender, brown-haired man with a weak face and watery blue eyes.

'There is a difference between caution and cowardice.' Irritation thickened the Creole's accent. 'But perhaps you are too stupid to see that, Simon.'

Coltrane gave no sign of feeling anger at the jibe. He just went on grinning as he poured tequila.

Jennings said: 'So someone cut Rafe. He had enough enemies. It don't mean we hafta call it off.'

'Rafe was the only one the Mexicans knew,' DuPré argued. 'Why should they believe us without him?'

'Because we'll be there,' husked Jennings. 'I got the details from Rafe a while back. They change the place every time, so we'd not have reason to be there less'n we knew about it. I'll pin Rafe's star on an' we tell 'em I'm the new marshal.'

'I'd still like to know who killed Rafe.' DuPré shook his head. 'It troubles me, that.'

'You been listening to too many stories,' Jennings said. 'It coulda been anyone.'

'A big man?' the Creole filled his glass, his eyes thoughtful. 'Brown hair? Metal where his left hand should be? Is that *anyone*?'

'You're seein' ghosts.' Jennings shrugged again. 'You think he'd come after us? A goddam blacksmith? Fer chrissakes, Jean! We bust his hand so bad he's most likely bled to death.'

'It is strange, though.' DuPré stared moodily into his glass. 'Wyatt had brown hair. And he was a big man. Do you remember which hand it was you smashed?'

Jennings shook his head.

'His left,' said DuPré. 'And in Terlingua they said the stranger had no left hand. Just metal. Blades, Vance! And Rafe was cut with blades.'

'You're crazy.' Jennings sneered. 'Wyatt's either dead or licking his wounds back in Black Rock.'

'But if he's alive?' the Creole asked. 'If it is him?'

'Then he's one man against the six of us.' Jennings' whisper got hoarser as he leant across the table to put his face close to the dark-haired man. 'Us down here. Andy an' Wade up in the hills.'

'Three down here,' DuPré corrected. 'And two in the hills. With me between if I go up there.'

'You sayin' you won't go?' Jennings eased back, his eyes hard on the Creole's face. 'You backin' out?'

'No.' DuPré weighed choices: the possibility of Tyler Wyatt waiting up for him against the certainty of Vance Jennings here and now. 'I'm not backing out. But I don't like it.'

'You'll like it a whole lot better when we've got that silver.' Jennings adjusted the bandanna around his throat. 'That much can buy a whole lot o' peace o' mind.'

'I hope so.' DuPré smoothed his hair down. 'I hope you are right, Vance.'

'You believe it.' Jennings grinned, thinking about the silver. 'You just do it like I said.'

The Creole nodded. 'Sure, Vance. Like you said.'

'He's scared,' Coltrane offered. 'He don't like goin' single-handed.'

Jennings husked laughter. 'If it is Wyatt, that should even 'em up. We left him kinda single-handed.'

Chapter Two

Tyler Wyatt had always been a patient man. Patient and determined.

It had taken patience to get his smithy started, to build a house for his wife. It had taken determination to resist the offers made by Cole Garrett, Josie's father, to help him out. Wyatt had a streak of stubborn independence, and that had prompted him to refuse Garrett's loans, to wait until he could offer Josie a home belonging to no one but them, built solely with his own efforts. He had waited, though, determined to do things his own way, and Josie had respected him for that. And so had Cole. The Southerner was the wealthiest man in Black Rock, what money he had saved from the ravaged Southland parlayed up to build the saloon he had called The Belle, after his dead wife. He had entertained plans to start a bank, to make Black Rock a thriving community.

And Wyatt had accepted an offer then. It had seemed too good to refuse: fifty dollars for a few nights' work. It had seemed simple. Cole had undertaken to hold three thousand dollars of stage company money for five days, and he had offered Wyatt ten dollars a night to guard the safe. Wyatt had accepted. And on the second night Vance Jennings and his gang had hit the town.

Wyatt's mouth tightened in a thin, hard line as the memories flooded back. Unconsciously, he raised his left arm, staring at the metal hand, the random light that filtered through the branches of the pine reflecting off the polished blades. Light flickered over his face, sparkling on his eyes. Reminding him.

They had lured the inhabitants of the little settlement out into the night by the simple expedient of ringing the town's fire bell. At gunpoint, they had herded everyone inside the fresh-built chapel. Every man, woman and child in Black Rock. Except for Cole Garrett and Josie and Wyatt himself.

He had been asleep, locked in Garrett's quarters with the stage money when the fire bell had woken him. He had come out to find Jennings holding a pistol on Garrett. And then he had been tied down, forced to hear why Jennings had come to Black Rock.

It hadn't been the money alone. That had started the raid, but then Jennings had discovered a bonus. An old debt he intended to settle in blood. Wyatt had been forced to listen as the outlaw explained.

Cole Garrett had ridden with Mosby during the War Between The States. Vance Jennings had been a youngster in a Kansas town called Allandale. Mosby had led an attack on the town, reprisal for the redleg massacre of a wagon train of refugees. During the fighting Jennings had seen his redleg uncle go down, and attacked the Confederate lieutenant wielding the sabre. Cole Garrett had reacted instinctively: his sword had gashed Jennings' throat, leaving the Kansan with a scar and a permanent whisper to remind him. When he had heard Garrett was living in Black Rock he had added personal revenge to his motives for the raid.

Wyatt had been forced to watch as the outlaw slowly butchered Garrett.

Worse, he had been forced to watch as one-by-one they raped Josie.

He could see her face now, blue eyes staring at him as though pain and horror and shame set her teetering on the brink of madness. And he had pulled away. He had seen her blonde hair tangled and sweaty; the blood on her thighs, on her buttocks; the outlaws' spillings smeared about her mouth. And he had failed to hide the revulsion: she had seen it in his eyes and gone frightened into some place inside her mind. She had brought a gun to him, but he had not used it, waiting for a better opportunity. He had hidden the pistol in their cabin when Jennings called for him to shoe their horses. And Josie had found it. And in her madness she had come out with the old hogleg Dragoon in both hands.

And the outlaws had blown her away.

Wyatt had gone crazy then. There was a hammer in his left hand, and he had swung it at Jennings' head. The blow had missed, and Jennings had taken revenge. He had pounded Wyatt's hand to a bloody ruin.

There had been a doctor in Black Rock, Doc Mortimer, and he had saved Wyatt's life. Saved his life, but not his hand. For that, there was no saving. Mortimer had amputated, and when Wyatt emerged again from unconsciousness, the doctor had seen a different man. Rage had curdled in Wyatt, had become a force that drove him to near-inhuman limits. He had waited out the healing of his stump and then set about constructing the metal hand he now wore. He had honed his natural talent with pistol and long gun to a deadly finesse, the fury pushing him, driving him until he was a lethal killing machine. Jennings had let slip that a stage guard, Tansy Moran, was the one put him onto the money. Wyatt had shut himself in a room alone with the man. Alone, save for the Bowie knife he carried. When he had emerged, he knew that Jennings was headed for the border town of Terlingua, where the marshal turned a blind eye to outlaw business.

Wyatt had quit Black Rock then. He had ridden down to Terlingua, where the marshal, Rafe Coombes, had tried to ambush him. That had been the first time Wyatt used the metal hand. Coombes had told him where Andy Chance and Wade Martin were holed up. And now they were both dead, and Wyatt waited patiently for Jean DuPré to show.

He lowered the gleaming metal, eyes narrowing as he fought back the pain that always came with the rage. There was hate in him, yes. He was determined to kill the outlaws; determined that they should know why they were dying. But with the hate there was also the pain of guilt. If he had not drawn back from Josie. If he had used the Dragoon she had smuggled to him instead of waiting. If he had not hidden the gun.

Lines creased his face as he fought the pain, pushing it back, down deep inside him. And gradually it was replaced with fury. A cold, implacable rage that lent him patience, that hardened his determination. He felt it still him, his body relaxing back against the pine as his eyes fastened again on the entrance to the bowl.

He could wait: all he had was time.

Behind him the bay stallion he had taken from Coombes cropped grass, tail switching lazily at the flies buzzing about its haunches. Wyatt lifted a canteen, sipping spring water. The sun was past its noonday zenith now, beyond the demarcation line of the pine tree's branches so that he was fully in shadow. He corked the canteen, wondering idly how much longer he would wait before DuPré showed.

It was mid-afternoon. The sun was shifted beyond the tip of the pine, pooling shadow over the downswing of the ridge. Beyond the cottonwoods, the hacienda was outlined with light, the peeling adobe plaster of the frontage glowing a creamy yellow, veined with the darkness of cracks. What little glass was left unbroken in the windows glittered, dust forming a reflective surface patched with black where the panes were missing. The spring shone silvery, the white drift of cloud mirrored on its surface. The grass was a brilliant green, speckled with little flowers of yellow and red and blue. The place appeared tranquil, undisturbed by the corpses rotting inside the ruined building or by the man on the ridge, waiting there to kill again.

Wyatt heard the horse coming through the entrance. A shoe clattered on stone and a pony snickered. In the corral behind the building the two penned animals looked up, nostrils flaring as they whinnied a reply. Wyatt lifted to his feet, right hand clamping over the stallion's nose as the big head came up. The stallion grunted, then returned to its grazing as the man turned away.

The rider was in sight now, moving slowly across the grass towards the hacienda. He was mounted on a buckskin gelding, the stock of a Winchester protruding from the saddle scabbard. He wore black pants tucked inside polished black boots, silver spurs gleaming on the heels. A black vest covered a white shirt, the collar fastened fastidiously, decorated with a black string tie despite the heat. There was a gunbelt around his waist, the holster dragged round to the left hip for riding so that Wyatt saw the Smith & Wesson Russian jutting from the leather. A flat brimmed black hat shaded the face, but Wyatt knew it would be good-looking, moustached. Knew the rider had to be Jean DuPré.

He waited until the Creole was past the stand of cottonwoods, then came down the ridge at a run. He moved fast across the space between the ridge and trees, ducking into the cottonwoods' shadow as DuPré shouted, 'Wade! Andy! *C'est moi*. It is Jean.'

When there was no reply, DuPré circled the corner of the building, checking the animals in the corral. Wyatt flattened against the bole of a cottonwood, waiting for him to come back into sight. When he did, the man with the metal hand could see his handsome face set in a frown. He halted to one side of the door and swung clear of the saddle. The Smith & Wesson was in his right hand, the hammer going back under the pressure of his thumb. He moved closer to the door, voice carrying on the still air.

'Wade? Andy? Are you there?'

Wyatt could hear the doubt in the Creole's tones. It brought a slight, cold smile to his face.

DuPré lifted a foot, kicking the door open, and went through into the shadowy room beyond. Wyatt came out from the trees, running for the wall. He reached the adobe and flattened against the warm plaster. Inside, he could hear DuPré gasp, muttering to himself in a mixture of languages.

'*Sacre Dieu!* Like Rafe. *Merde! C'est* Wyatt. I told Vance.'

Wyatt crossed the window and halted inside the frame of the door. He had a Colt's Peacemaker in his right hand, the muzzle set square on DuPré's back. The Creole was standing with the Smith & Wesson dangling at his side, his body seeming frozen in an attitude of shock as his head moved slowly from side to side, studying the corpses.

Wade Martin lay with his knees drawn up close to his chest. His arms were folded across his midriff and his chin was tucked down as though he nursed a pain in his belly. Before he died, he had been: Wyatt had shot him in the stomach. There was dried blood in a wide circle around the body, more on the shirt under the black covering of flies. Scavengers had torn flesh from the buttocks, and ribs showed white where a hole had been ripped in his side. Andy Chance looked worse. He rested on his back, wrists and ankles bound. Blood covered the face, the cuts imparted by Wyatt's metal hand opened wider by the scavengers. The eye sockets were empty, staring in fly-clustered ruin at the ceiling; maggots writhed between the parted lips. There was a hole in the front of the body, insects busy within. The hole was where the heart should have been.

DuPré shook his head. And Wyatt said:

'You make a move an' I'll blow a hole in your back.'

The Creole stiffened. Wyatt could see his fingers tense on the pistol. He said: 'Lower the hammer, then drop the gun.'

DuPré eased the hammer down and let the Smith & Wesson drop to the floor.

'Kick it back here.'

DuPré set a boot on the pistol and sent it skidding over

the dusty boards. Wyatt stooped down, not taking the Colt off the Creole's back, and hooked the gun up. He flung his arm out, hurling the weapon onto the balcony at the rear of the room. It rattled on ancient planks, dust spilling in thick streamers onto the floor.

'It is the blacksmith, *n'est-ce pas*?' DuPré's voice was heavily accented now; thick with tension. 'You are Tyler Wyatt.'

'Damn' right I am.' Wyatt's own voice was harsh. 'Turn around slow.'

The Creole turned, his face visibly pale. He licked his lips, dark eyes moving from the Colt in Wyatt's hand to the man's eyes. He saw no mercy there.

'You are going to kill me like this?' he asked. 'Unarmed?'

'How you killed Cole Garrett,' Wyatt said, ice in his voice. 'How you killed my wife.'

'Vance killed Garrett.' DuPré shrugged slightly. 'Your wife? She was firing a pistol. I fired back. Like the others.'

'Two of them are dead.' Wyatt smiled. And DuPré swallowed hard, raw fear knotting in his throat. 'You're the third.'

'And you are no better than us,' said DuPré; quickly. 'To shoot an unarmed man is no better than what Vance did.'

The smile on Wyatt's face got uglier. He shook his head slightly.

'I'm not shooting you.' He said slowly, the words cutting through the buzzing of the flies. 'You gave me this. I'm going to kill you with it.'

The Creole's eyes followed the movement of the big man's left arm. They fastened on the metal hand, on the gleaming tines set there. Sweat beaded on his forehead, trickling down his face so that he blinked.

'In Black Rock you carried a knife.' Wyatt eased the hammer of the Colt down. Holstered the pistol. 'You still got it?'

DuPré nodded, only his head moving. Wyatt said, 'Good. Bring it out.'

The moustached man reached behind his back, right hand emerging with a blade extended from his fist. It was five or six inches long, about one inch wide, tapering to a point with both edges honed to razor sharpness. He held it with the casual expertise of a knife fighter, thumb against the quillon to set one cutting edge uppermost. Wyatt tugged his belt buckle open and tossed the rig out through the door.

'I'm going to kill you.' The way he said it sounded like a death sentence. 'For what you did to Josie. An' to Cole. An' me.'

DuPré shrugged, wiping sweat from his moustache as his knees bent, right arm thrusting forwards, left moving out to the side, away from his body. Wyatt imitated the movement, the arm positions reversed so that the vicious tines jutting from the metal fist pointed out towards the Creole's face.

'You'll talk,' he said; confidently. 'Before you die, you'll tell me where Jennings aims to hit the silver train.'

DuPré's brows arched and a faint smile showed teeth below his moustache.

'Perhaps. Perhaps not.'

He came forwards as he said it, moving crab-like over the dusty floor with the knife weaving before him. Wyatt circled, putting his body between DuPré and the door. The man seemed to have gained confidence from the knife, as though he felt himself at an advantage, superior in this kind of fighting. He feinted to the right, and as Wyatt shifted position to cover the movement, the knife swung suddenly back, dropping to cut in below his guard. The big man sucked in breath, bending over the swing so that the blade cut air less than an inch from his midriff.

DuPré grunted, the smile set like a rictus on his face. He moved back, drawing Wyatt farther into the room, the blade never ceasing its constant motion, shafts of sunlight glinting off the steel. Wyatt followed him, eyes as restless as the Creole's blade. They flickered from the knife to the man's face, to his feet, to his arm, seeking indication of the next attack, assessing DuPré. Then, almost without warning, the Creole jumped forwards. His blade darted at Wyatt's throat, prompting an instinctive defence. Wyatt brought the metal hand up, cutting at the moustached man's wrist. But DuPré's arm was no longer there. Instead, it dropped past the tines, the knife driving for Wyatt's belly. The big man turned, twisting his body to present a narrower target. He felt pain as the blade cut through his shirt, glancing over ribs. Then satisfaction as he turned his own arm, using the pivoting motion of his body to rake the tines down the Creole's bicep. Three long slashes showed in the material of DuPré's shirt, pale skin briefly visible before crimson coloured the paleness. DuPré winced, hacking back at Wyatt's belly as he moved away.

'Perhaps it is you who will die,' he murmured. 'Perhaps I will kill you.'

'No.' Wyatt's teeth showed in a feral grin. 'Not me.'

As he spoke he moved closer, turning his left arm so that the metal hand lifted up, the cutting edges of the tines uppermost, curving towards the Creole's groin. DuPré danced backwards. Wyatt followed him. Abruptly, DuPré cut at his chest in a feinting move that was intended to turn Wyatt, to present his unguarded side. But Wyatt didn't turn. Instead, he brought his left arm up as though punching, leaning back from DuPré's attack. The tines grated on the knife blade, trapping it. Wyatt twisted his wrist, closing the distance between them as he felt the Creole's arm bend. DuPré fastened his left hand on Wyatt's forearm, fighting to ease the pressure so that he could drag his blade free. Wyatt hit him hard in the ribs, gusting wind from between the clenched teeth. His face was close to DuPré's, and he saw the confidence go out of the Creole's eyes as he punched again. DuPré grunted, loosing his grip on Wyatt's arm and jumping back to drag the knife free.

Wyatt ducked under a cut, raking the metal hand fast over the man's belly. The cloth of the vest ripped, but DuPré was moving back too fast for the blow to score flesh. Moving back exactly as Wyatt intended. Moving back towards the corner of the room, where his movements would be hampered by the angles of the walls.

DuPré saw the danger as the metal hand darted again at his face. He avoided the blow, seeking to spin Wyatt and escape from the corner, but the big man moved too fast. He came sideways, blocking the Creole with the metal hand slamming sparks from the knife as steel clashed on steel. For an instant, DuPré's arm was lifted, extended to its full length. Wyatt bent his knees, coming under the arm with his right shoulder smashing into the Creole's chest. The man was hurled back against the angle of the walls, pinned there by Wyatt's greater weight as the brown-haired man lifted his right arm, hand clamping on DuPré's wrist.

Wyatt came up to his full height. DuPré's arm was dragged out, the underside turned upwards, Wyatt's shoulder a pivot between elbow and armpit. Wyatt held his grip on the wrist, ignoring the pounding of DuPré's fist as he lifted his left arm. The Creole saw the danger and grabbed a handful of Wyatt's thick hair. The big man felt his scalp stretch as his head was yanked back, but the metal hand was coming down now, unstoppable. The tines smashed onto DuPré's wrist. Sliced, driven deep by the power in Wyatt's blow. The shirt cuff parted, beneath the material, the skin. Three red maws appeared, the taut surface skin peeling back in grinning crimson mouths. DuPré screamed as the veins cut through. Screamed again as blood spurted from the wounds. His fingers, nerveless, opened to let the knife fall to the floor, close to the corpse of Wade Martin. Wyatt let go his hold, spinning away as droplets of blood spattered his face.

DuPré ignored the knife. His left hand clutched his severed wrist, fingers probing in a desperate attempt to stem the blood flow. Crimson tinted his neatly-trimmed nails, gouted thick between his fingers. Wyatt was still smiling as he slashed the hand over the Creole's face. He felt the blades grate on bone and as DuPré's jaw yawned wide in a scream, teeth showed through the gaps in his cheek, more crimson fountaining out to soak his shirt.

'*Cher Dieu!*' He shook his head in disbelief, blood spraying in a wide arc with the movement. 'Ah, *merde!*'

'Jennings!' Wyatt snarled. 'Where do you meet him?'

DuPré looked up. Blood curtained his cheek, ragged flesh hanging in tatters. He spat blood.

'I am dying, *mon ami*. Why should I tell you anything?'

Wyatt answered the question with a sudden movement of his arm. The metal hand flashed forwards, the points of the tines driving between DuPré's legs. The Creole's eyes opened horribly wide as sharpened steel sliced into his testicles. He screamed again, but now it was a very thin, shrill sound. He went down on his knees, staring at the blood staining the front of his pants.

'I can make it last,' Wyatt said. 'I can make it last a long time. Like them.'

DuPré turned his head as Wyatt pointed at the corpses. His face was emptied of colour, except where the crimson decorated his cheek and jaw. His eyes clamped tight shut, then opened again, white showing all around the pupils. Blood and spittle frothed on his lips.

'There is a ford,' he said quickly. 'A place called Tres Pinos. They meet the silver there. It is a few miles south from Terlingua.'

Wyatt took hold of the man's hair, hauling him upright. DuPré slumped against the wall, his breathing ragged, his features made ugly with pain.

'How many?' Wyatt demanded.

'Three.' The Creole groaned. 'Vance, Coltrane and

Strother Cannon. I was to bring the others to cover from behind.'

His eyes turned again towards the corpses as he said it. He licked his lips.

'Not like them. Please? Not like that.'

'The money you took from Black Rock.' Wyatt turned the face back with the tips of the tines. 'Where is it?'

'Terlingua,' moaned DuPré. 'There is a bank.'

'Good,' Wyatt said. 'That's real good.'

And drove his left arm forwards in a punch that hit the Creole directly in the groin. The tines drove deep, slicing the soft flesh. DuPré screeched, doubling over the blow. The metal hand came away bloody, tatters of cloth and little pieces of puckered flesh adhering to the blades. Wyatt watched as the man went down writhing, the screeching, shrieking sound filling the room. DuPré forgot his severed wrist as he pressed both hands tight against the agony burning through his insides. Blood pumped between his fingers, drenching his pants. It pooled between his kicking legs, sweet-smelling and sickly, cut through with the acrid stench of his opened bowels. Flies buzzed towards him, drawing closer as his writhing grew less frantic, slowing as the crimson pulsed less fiercely from groin and arm.

After a while the flow eased, faltering to a spasmodic welling that died away with the shrieking. The Creole's eyes rolled up, pupils and iris replaced by white. A harsh rattling cry trembled from his throat and he was still. The flies closed in.

Wyatt stared at the ruined body. There was a glint of savage satisfaction in his eyes as he murmured,

'I said you'd lose. You just don't have the balls.'

Chapter Three

Wyatt thought about his next move as he rode away from the hacienda. Vance Jennings wouldn't miss DuPré and the others until they failed to show up at Tres Pinos. He would be expecting them to join in the fight from behind, but with the Creole, Wade Martin and Andy Chance all dead, Jennings and his two remaining men would be going up against a squad of *federales*. The odds would be against the outlaws, and Wyatt didn't like that. He didn't like it for the simple reason that the Mexicans would most likely gun down the three Americans. And Wyatt didn't want that. He wanted to kill them himself; to let them know who was killing them.

He came down the dusk-darkened trail towards the lights of Villalta trying to work out a solution. He could maybe reach the ford before the silver shipment arrived. Set up his own ambush. But that was risky: it depended on Jennings and Coltrane and Cannon showing themselves before the *federales* came within earshot, and it could force him to kill at long range. He didn't want that. He wanted it to be up close. Close enough that he could see their faces as they died, let them see his. And that meant somehow diverting the silver to leave Jennings and the others waiting at the ford.

He decided on a way as the lights got brighter and the smells of cooking food reminded him it was a long time since he'd eaten better than hardtack and jerky.

Villalta was built along a fold of the hills, hugging the flank with the land dropping away steeply in front of the pueblo. The buildings were adobe and slate, cut hard against the rock face with the trail widening out to form a tiny plaza. There was a fountain at the centre of the square, its stone slimed green with the steady trickle of water dribbling from the chipped carving, the overspill running away down a paved channel. A cantina and a small hotel stood side by side, facing across the plaza to the *rurale* station, where the Mexican flag hung motionless in the still night air. Beyond the *rurale* station there was a small church, its tower jutting against the sky, the ground beyond busy with ornate tombstones. The third side of the plaza held a livery stable, the fourth a hardware store and a general store. At an angle to the main trail there was a secondary road cut up into the hills, leading to the mineworkings that Wyatt could see casting a dull red glow into the night. The moon was a pale half disc, shining yellow-silver on the pines covering the upper slopes, reflecting off the tiled roofs and the stark white of the buildings. There were lights showing in the houses, more spilling over the plaza from the cantina and the hotel, a lantern burning inside the *rurale* station.

Wyatt rode slow across the square, ignoring the men who lounged on the porch fronting the cantina, the solitary *rurale* slumped with his rifle between his knees on a chair before the station. He halted in front of the livery and swung to the ground as an old man with a battered straw sombrero pulled down over a face that seemed more lines than skin came out with an anticipatory smile on his mouth.

The smile disappeared as he saw Wyatt's left hand, replaced by an expression of nervous curiosity.

'*Su mano*,' he gaped. '*Es metálico. Una garra.*'

Wyatt grinned. *Una garra* – a claw. It was as good a description as any for the weapon he had forged to replace his hand.

'*Si*,' he nodded. '*Una garra. Pero mi dinero es bueno.*'

The old man shrugged, eyes still held by the metal hand. Wyatt passed him the reins and took coin from his pocket. The jingle brought the oldster's gaze up, his face creasing in a smile again as he saw the silver glint in the moonlight.

'One night,' Wyatt said. 'Go easy on the oats.'

He dragged his saddlebags onto his shoulder and slid the Winchester from the scabbard, striding away across the plaza with the old man staring after him, a puzzled look on his face. Before very long, Wyatt knew, word would spread through the pueblo: there was a *yanqui* ridden in with metal where his left hand should be. *Una garra*. He would be pointed out, watched by the kids, men would ask him what had happened. It was a thing he was going to have to get used to.

He went into the hotel. It was a two-storey adobe building with a wood balcony running along the front. The vestibule was tiled, his boots ringing loud on the stone, waking the clerk dozing behind the desk. The man turned sleepy eyes on the stranger, automatically shifting a register to face Wyatt.

'*Buenas noches*.' He hadn't seen the hand yet. '*Quieren habitacione*?'

'*Si*.' Wyatt propped the Winchester against the desk-front and scrawled his name in the book. 'For one night. You got a bath?'

The clerk nodded, passing Wyatt a key as the American dropped money onto the scarred surface of the desk.

'You will eat, *señor*?'

'A lot.' Wyatt nodded again. 'An' send a bottle up with the water.'

'*Claro!* We have American whiskey.'

'That's good.' Wyatt lifted the Winchester, turning for the stairs. 'That's real good.'

The clerk saw the metal hand for the first time as the big man crossed the vestibule. His mouth dropped open and he fought back the gasp of surprise rising in his throat. *Madre de Dios!* What would the gringos think of next? To replace a hand with a thing like that. A thing more weapon than anything else. Like the claws of a *tigre*.

Wyatt heard the clerk's grunt and ignored it as he climbed the stairs and followed the corridor along to his room. It was at the front of the building, high windows opening onto the balcony overlooking the plaza. He tugged the shutters closed before lighting the lantern suspended from the centre of the ceiling. The glow outlined a small room, faded carpet covering the planks of the floor. The walls were rough-plastered adobe, a spider's web draped across one corner, the only other decoration a religious painting hung above the bed. The bed was pushed up against the wall, brass head and curlicued foot tarnished, the sheets well-darned but clean. There was a wash-stand beside the bed, a cloth-covered jug standing in a chipped bowl. On the wall facing the bed there was a row of wooden hooks.

Wyatt hung his hat on one hook and tossed his saddlebags onto the bed. The springs creaked as he sat down and he saw a cockroach scurry over the carpet to the safety of a crack in the wall. He took off his gunbelt, checking the Peacemaker before draping the belt over the bedhead, then began to ease his boots off. It was difficult with only one good hand – one more of the many small things he was adjusting to. He had the left boot off when there was a tapping on the door and a voice called, '*Su baño, señor.*' Automatically, he reached for the Colt, pointing the gun at the door as he called back, '*Bueno*. Bring it in.'

The door opened and a man in a dirty white tunic came through with a tub held on his back like a turtle shell. He looked at the pistol in Wyatt's right hand, then at the metal of his left. He set the tub down with a hurried thud and slid past the second man who came in with two big buckets of steaming water and a bottle of whiskey. The second man stared nervously at Wyatt as he filled the tub, then darted out the door muttering something about fetching cold water. Wyatt dropped the Colt back inside the holster, waiting until buckets of cold water, soap and a big, rough towel were brought. He called the last man back and had him haul off the other boot, grinning at the way he couldn't take his eyes off the metal hand.

Then he locked the door and stripped. He loosened the

fastenings of the metal hand and dropped the appendage on the bed. The thing was built to cover the stump of his wrist, like an inverted cup, the inside padded where it settled on the hardened scar tissue of the amputation. The flesh there was calloused, toughened by use now so that there was little of the rawness he had first experienced. He stared at the stump, remembering the pain as the hammer had descended, pounding the bones to shattered fragments, the flesh to bloody pulp. Then he smiled as he looked at the claws extending from the metal and remembered what they could do. He reached for the bottle, lifting the shot glass that covered the open neck, and poured a measure. The whiskey tasted good, burning down his throat to settle in a warm pool in his belly. He drank a second, then set glass and bottle close by the tub before climbing into the hot water.

He lay there, not thinking about anything as the water discoloured, then scrubbed himself with the coarse soap and upended both buckets of cold water over his head. He dried himself, then rubbed some of the linament Doc Mortimer had given him into the stump of his wrist. An idea was taking shape in his mind, one that might just bring Jennings and the other two within reach of the claws.

He was smiling again as he buttoned a clean shirt over his muscular chest and prepared to go find something to eat.

The dining room that occupied most of the hotel's lower floor was busy. Wyatt found a table down to one end, set in the angle of the walls. It was empty and after a while the Mexicans stopped talking about his hand and went back to their eating. A girl with big, dark eyes came out with a bowl of guacamole and a platter of tacos, and the American began to spoon up the rich pasty mixture, washing it down with spring water from the jug the girl set on the table. She came back with chili and tortillas. Wyatt cleaned the dish and sat back, sipping bitter black coffee.

The moon was moved farther across the sky when he went out onto the plaza again and the guitars strumming in the cantina were louder. Moths fluttered in the still, warm air, describing suicidal arcs about the lanterns hung from the verandahs. Bats swept through the darkness. Wyatt went over to the *rurale* station.

The guard looked at him, not bothering to rise, a cheroot hanging from the left corner of his mouth.

'El jefe?' Wyatt asked. *'Donde es?'*

The glowing tip of the cheroot lifted to point at the cantina: *'Allá'*.

'Gracias.' Wyatt turned away, heading for the bright-lit door.

Smoke filled the air inside the cantina, wreathing under the low ceiling like mist rising from dawn-damp bottomland. It came close to overpowering the odour of cheap liquor and sweat. Close, but not quite. At the far end of the room three men in big, curly-brimmed sombreros were plucking guitar strings as a woman with long, night-black hair husked out a plaintive song about unrequited love. Men sat at tables or clustered along the bar, their concentration focused on the singer so that few noticed Wyatt's deformity as he pushed through the crowd and called for tequila. A barkeep with hair pomaded flat across a square skull put a bottle in front of him and flourished a dirty-looking cloth at a glass. Wyatt dropped coin on the wooden surface and dragged a plate of salt with slices of lemon set around the rim closer to his right hand. The tequila stung his mouth as he swallowed, then sent a line of fire coursing down his throat. He took a pinch of salt and bit into a segment of lemon, grateful for the taste after the rawness of the liquor.

He beckoned the barkeep closer and asked, *'El jefe de rurales es aquí?'*

'Seguro.' The barkeep nodded. 'Juan is always here. He is in love.'

He pointed towards the guitarists. 'The one with the beard.'

Wyatt looked down the room. A line of chairs was drawn up in a semicircle before the musicians. They were occupied by men in the dun-coloured tunics of the rural police, their heads bare as though in respect for the entertainers. There were nine of them, at their centre a thin-faced man with carefully-trimmed hair and a neat, black beard.

'He would not thank you for interrupting him.' The barkeep's warning halted Wyatt's movement. 'The last time anyone interrupted Rosita, Juan had him flogged.'

Wyatt grunted and drank more tequila, waiting for the music to end.

The song came to a throaty conclusion. The guitars strummed a final, descending chord. The *rurale* captain led the clapping as the woman dropped a curtsey that exposed a large expanse of brown cleavage and turned in a swirl of skirts to disappear through a door at the rear. The *rurales* stood up and Wyatt saw that the captain equalled his own six feet plus, though without the heavy muscling that bulked out the American. He began to move through the crowd.

'Capitán?' He looked into moist black eyes set in a hawkish face, the features arrogant, their hardness emphasized by the thrust of the close-trimmed beard. 'I'd like to speak with you.'

'Then speak.' The man replied in perfect American, no accent thickening his tone. 'But swiftly. I have business to attend.'

He stared at Wyatt with an expression close to boredom. Then the languid gaze focused on the American's metal hand and boredom was replaced with surprise. A hint of interest.

Wyatt smiled, thinking it was one way to draw attention.

'It's about the silver,' he said. 'You could have trouble.'

The *rurale* captain studied him with an expression of suspicion mingling with the arrogance.

'Speak,' he said.

'Here?' Wyatt gestured around the crowded cantina. 'There are too many ears.'

The Mexican sniffed, toying with the peak of his cap. Then: 'Very well. Follow me.'

He said it like a man not used to having his orders ignored, settling his cap over his neat hair and marching down the cantina without checking to see if Wyatt was following him. The big man shrugged slightly and stepped into the gap left by the *capitán*'s passage, conscious of the eyes turned his way now, as though his conversation with the *rurale* officer had made him a figure of some importance. He pushed through the bead curtain covering the door and stepped onto the verandah.

'We will talk in my office,' the Mexican said, curtly. 'Come.'

Wyatt fell into step beside him, crossing the plaza back to the *rurale* station.

This time, the guard outside rose to his feet, shifting his rifle to his shoulder to execute a sloppy salute. The captain snapped off a crisp reply and pushed the door open. Wyatt followed him into a wide, tile-floored hall lit by two lanterns hung on chains from the ceiling. There was a staircase leading up to an internal balcony that ran around three sides of the room, and doors set in the walls. The captain went up the stairs like a man in a hurry, bootheels ringing metalically on the marble surface. He opened a door facing the stairhead and motioned Wyatt inside as he struck a match to light the lamp set to one side of a paper-littered desk. The yellow glow outlined a room decorated with military precision. On the wall behind the desk a flag was nailed to the adobe, the eagle and snake emblem of Mexico dominating the room. Shutters were closed over the window to the left, and on the right wall there was a locked gun rack, bolt action Mannlicher carbines behind the glass. Either side of the rack sabres hung crossed.

'I am Captain Juan Rodrigo.' The Mexican sat down in a big, leather-bound chair. 'You are?'

'Wyatt.' He took the chair Rodrigo pointed at, settling his hat on his knee. 'Tyler Wyatt.'

'Tyler Wyatt.' Rodrigo said it slowly, nodding as though the name was familiar. 'What do you wish to tell me about the silver, Wyatt?'

He took off his cap, setting it on the desk and brushing his hair smooth. He seemed vaguely bored.

'You're due to escort a shipment to the border,' Wyatt said. 'The marshal out of Terlingua was to meet you at a crossing called Tres Pinos.'

Interest replaced the boredom. Rodrigo lifted a hand, silencing Wyatt.

'*Was?*' he said. 'You put it in the past?'

'He is,' Wyatt answered. 'He's dead.'

Rodrigo nodded thoughtfully. Then: 'How do you know he is – *lo siento*, was – to meet me at Tres Pinos?'

'A man told me,' Wyatt said. 'A man called Jean DuPré.'

'DuPré?' The Mexican shrugged. 'I do not know this name. He is a Frenchman?'

'A Creole,' Wyatt replied. 'He's past tense, too. Passed on.'

Rodrigo lifted an ornate paperknife from the desk and began to turn it in his hands. Wyatt noticed that his fingers were very long, delicate-looking. The blade sent little shafts of light dancing over the room. Rodrigo's face was impassive as he said:

'So far there are two dead men in your story, *señor* Wyatt. And you know of a place only myself and Marshal Coombes should know about. I think you had better explain.'

'What I'm tryin' to do,' Wyatt retorted, feeling irritation at the *rurale* officer's bland arrogance. 'To warn you.'

Rodrigo smiled tightly and gestured for him to continue.

'Coombes was crooked,' Wyatt said. 'He was working with DuPré.'

'Common knowledge,' Rodrigo interrupted. 'Marshal Coombes liked to butter his bread on both sides. But he did not interfere with the silver shipments. That was too big a thing for a worm like him.'

'Not this time.' Wyatt shrugged, watching the captain's face. 'I don't know how much that silver is worth, but Coombes was plannin' to take it. Him and a bunch of outlaws headed by a man called Jennings. Vance Jennings. DuPré was one of the gang. That's how I know about Tres Pinos.'

'You killed them?' Rodrigo's smile got a little wider. Then he shook his head. 'It does not matter. What you *yanquis* do on your side of the border is no concern of mine. Please continue – this outlaw called Jennings was planning to take the silver.'

'*Is*, this time,' Wyatt corrected. 'Coombes is dead, but Jennings still plans to hit you at Tres Pinos.'

'How many men does he have?' Rodrigo's smile flattened. He dropped the paperknife and stroked his beard. 'I lead a detachment of twelve men.'

'He's got enough,' Wyatt lied. 'More than enough to take you. He'll be waitin' up at the ford. Ready to ambush you.'

'I see.' Rodrigo looked hard into Wyatt's eyes. 'Why do you tell me this?'

Wyatt shrugged. 'Figgered it was my duty.'

The Mexican went on staring at him. Then: 'Why should you concern yourself with Mexican silver, *señor* Wyatt? I think you must have some personal interest at stake here.'

Wyatt glanced down at his metal hand and decided to take a chance: somehow he had to persuade Rodrigo to take another route than the Tres Pinos crossing. He raised his arm so that the metal hand reflected lamp light. It glittered brighter than the paperknife.

'Jennings gave me this,' he said tautly. 'He smashed my hand. And he killed my wife. I don't want to see him get that much silver.'

No sympathy showed on the Mexican's face as he said, 'That is reason enough. You hunt this outlaw?'

Wyatt nodded.

Rodrigo said: 'And a man with all that silver could go a long way. Far enough to hide from you. You are afraid of losing him.'

It was close enough to the truth. It hadn't occurred to Wyatt that the silver would afford Jennings an escape: his concern had been solely that the outlaw might die under the *rurales'* guns. But it was logical. And it seemed like a lever he could use to persuade Rodrigo.

'That's right,' he said. 'I trailed them as far as Terlingua. Then I heard about their plan.'

'From Coombes,' murmured the officer. 'Before he died. Or from this man DuPré.'

'Yeah.' Wyatt nodded. 'But it all adds up to the same thing. Jennings is waiting for you at Tres Pinos.'

'Coombes was to take delivery there.' Rodrigo's hawkish features grew thoughtful. 'I have no authorization to cross the border. Yet the silver must be delivered to Terlingua.'

'You need authorization?' Wyatt asked.

Rodrigo nodded. 'I am a military man, *señor* Wyatt. I cannot come and go as I choose.'

'So get authorization,' Wyatt suggested. 'Then take it by another route.'

'That would take time.' The Mexican shook his head. 'And it is important that I reach the border on schedule.'

He smiled again as Wyatt frowned, adding: '*Señorita* Vasquez – the lady you doubtless saw in the cantina? – wishes to take a coach from there. I have promised her safe passage. Coombes was to escort her into Terlingua.'

Wyatt thought fast, seeing his plan falter.

'Look,' he said. 'Suppose I took her into town? I could put her on the stage. You could get your authorization an' bring the silver up later. That way everyone gets what they want.'

'Except this outlaw,' murmured Rodrigo. 'Jennings is left waiting for nothing.'

'He'll head back to Terlingua,' Wyatt said, smiling now. 'And I get what I want.'

Rodrigo answered his smile, glancing at the metal protruding from the American's shirt sleeve.

'Very well. We shall help one another. As you *yanquis* say, we will give one another a hand.'

Chapter Four

Rosita Vasquez had the kind of big, dark eyes that made men think about beds, and the kind of body that promised the bed wouldn't be for sleeping in. Even under the demure green travelling dress she wore, the contours of her figure were clear, breasts thrusting the material taut above a slender waist, hugging it tight over sensuous hips. As she stepped down onto the plaza, a froth of petticoat swirled about trim ankles encased in dark silk and her eyes laughed as she took in the appreciative stares of the watching men. Her hair was piled up on top of her head, a tiny hat with a silk tail pinned in place on the raven tumble. Her face was oval, dominated by the eyes, the nose perhaps a trifle too strong, but the generous mouth compensating for that.

Rodrigo took her elbow and escorted her decorously to the phaeton waiting by the fountain. He was wearing some kind of dress uniform, tan jodhpurs snugged into brown boots polished energetically enough that they reflected sunlight almost as brightly as the silver spurs on his heels, the chest of his tunic crossed by a brown leather strap fastening to the belt circling his narrow waist. A flapped holster was set on the right of the belt, a sabre was sheathed on the left. His cap shaded his face, insignia glinting above the brim. He gave off a faint odour of lavender water and metal polish.

Wyatt stood beside the phaeton, holding the reins of the bay stallion and feeling drab in comparison. It had been two days since he rode in to Villalta and by now he was feeling restless, eager to move on. The deal he had worked out with Rodrigo was simple: the *rurale* captain and his men would escort the wagon as far as the border, Wyatt would take it on to Terlingua. Jennings would be left waiting at the Tres Pinos crossing while Rodrigo organized some alternative route for the silver shipment, and before too long the outlaw had to realize something was wrong. The way Wyatt had it figured out, that would bring Jennings back to Terlingua. After that the man with the metal hand would just see how things worked out.

He doffed his hat as Rodrigo and the woman halted before him.

'*Señorita* Rosita Vasquez,' the Mexican said formally. '*Señor* Tyler Wyatt.'

'Ma'am?' Wyatt smiled at her, conscious of the slight frown that crossed Rodrigo's features as she answered his smile. 'I heard you in the cantina. You sing real nice.'

'*Gracias.*' She ducked her head in acknowledgement. 'Juan has told me you are to be my escort into America.'

'My pleasure.' Wyatt saw her eyes move to his metal hand and wondered what Rodrigo had told her about him. 'I hope it's a smooth journey.'

'It had better be.' There was the hint of a threat in the Mexican's voice. 'You will be responsible for precious cargo.'

'Juan.' The woman turned her smile on the officer. 'I am sure *señor* Wyatt is reliable. After all, you picked him.'

Rodrigo nodded curtly; Wyatt said nothing about their arrangement. Instead, he stood back as the officer handed the woman onto the phaeton then climbed up beside her. The springs creaked as he settled on the padded seat, and he waited for the woman to arrange her skirts before lifting the whip. Wyatt swung astride the bay stallion, glancing back at the *rurales* lining up in column of twos behind.

'*Vamos!*' Rodrigo's shout was echoed by the crack of the whip. The two horse team surged forwards, shoes clattering on the stones of the plaza. Wyatt touched heels to the stallion's flanks and the big horse trotted forwards, moving up alongside the wagon.

They went out of Villalta with the early morning sun bright on their faces.

'You think something's gone wrong?'

Simon Coltrane hunkered by the fire, pale eyes not quite looking at Jennings' face. The dark-haired man was honing the foreshortened blade of the sabre he had used on Cole Garrett, face expressionless as he passed the whetstone over the metal. On the far side of the flames Strother Cannon looked up from a skillet, scarred face interested.

When Jennings made no reply, Coltrane licked his lips and said: 'Vance? You think that maybe Jean was right?'

Jennings tested the sabre on his thumb, smiling tautly at the edge. He thrust the blade into the sheath on his belt and turned a cold-eyed stare on the brown-haired man.

'You gettin' worried, Simon?'

Coltrane shrugged. 'We been waitin' a time now.'

'An' we'll wait longer,' rasped Jennings. 'Long as we need to.'

'How long's that?' Coltrane didn't look at him as he said it.

'Until I decide we waited long enough.' Jennings hiked a bottle from his saddlebag and drew the cork with his teeth. Took a long swallow. 'That all right with you, Simon?'

Coltrane nodded hurriedly. 'Sure, Vance. Whatever you say.'

'That's right.' Jennings wiped his mouth. 'Whatever I say. Don't forget that, Simon.'

Yellow teeth showed in Cannon's mouth as he chuckled. Coltrane glanced at him, then away. He eyed the bottle, waiting for Jennings to pass it over. When it came, he drank fast, spilling liquor over his stubbled chin. He didn't say anything more.

Around them the night was dark, the sky a panoply of star-studded velvet with the thinning moon fighting for a place. The river gurgled softly, splashing over rocks and sand bars, surface silvered by the starlight. Giant saguarro thrust curving limbs towards the heavens, and where the bluff shaded down to the water, three big skeletal pines stood like sentinels, their branches old and bare and dead. Cannon began to fork slabs of deer meat onto tin plates, passing the first to Jennings. Like a wolf offering the pack leader first choice at a kill.

'I turn back in the morning.'

Juan Rodrigo shook a long, very black cheroot from a metal case and offered it to Wyatt. The big American took the smoke with a grunt of thanks and lifted a twig from the fire, lighting first the Mexican's, then his own tobacco.

'This is the border?' Wyatt glanced at the water running smooth between wide flanks of sand.

'Si.' Rodrigo nodded, smoke pluming lazy from his mouth. 'America starts on the far side. I have no authority there.'

'I'll take her through.' Wyatt looked at the wagon. A canopy was extended from one side, forming a tent. Rosita Vasquez was inside. 'Don't worry.'

'She is very important,' said Rodrigo. 'To me. You understand that?'

'Sure.' For an instant, Wyatt's face twisted in a grimace of pain. 'I know what it's like to care for someone.'

'That is good.' Rodrigo's face was lit red by the glowing tip of the cheroot as he inhaled. 'That is one of the reasons I trust you.'

'One?' queried the American.

'Yes.' Rodrigo nodded again. 'Another is that I do not think you are very interested in women. Not since . . .'

He turned his dark eyes towards Wyatt's metal hand, not finishing the sentence, just letting it hang there. Wyatt nodded, not speaking.

'There is a third,' Rodrigo said. 'Something you should remember if I am wrong about you.'

Wyatt waited, studying the man's hawkish features. Rodrigo smiled, white teeth showing through his beard.

'If anything happens to Rosita. Anything at all, *señor* Wyatt. If you harm her – or let her come to harm – then I shall forget about this border.' He gestured at the river, the cheroot trailing sparks behind his hand. 'I shall cross it and I shall kill you. Do not forget that.'

'I won't.' Wyatt shook his head.

'Good.' The Mexican climbed to his feet, tossing the half-smoked cheroot into the fire. 'We understand one another, I think.'

'I think we do,' Wyatt answered.

He watched as the Mexican strode over to the *rurale* pacing the bank, their low-voiced conversation indiscernible, and blew smoke in a long cloud that hung on the still, warm air. When the cheroot was smoked down to a stub, he ground it into the sand and stretched back against his saddle, pulling his blanket over his tall body. Somewhere in the distance a lone coyote called, the wailing cry seeming to echo off the sky. An owl drifted overhead, its flight silent, a white shape against the night. Wyatt let sleep take him.

He woke with the deceptive light of the false dawn brightening the mist coming off the river, shivering in the early morning chill as he kicked the fire to fresh life and added wood. Rodrigo sat up, yawning, brushing dew from his beard. He barked an order and a shape came out of the greyness, poncho bulked out by the rifle the guard was clutching. Rodrigo stood up, smoothing his uniform into place, and the guard began to wake the other *rurales*.

Coffee was bubbling in the pot before the woman woke and Rodrigo carried a mug over to the phaeton, ducking inside the canvas. The sun fought through the mist and suddenly full dawn drove off the darkness. Wyatt walked over to the river, moving clear of the camp before he unstrapped the metal hand and set it carefully down where a slab of stone reached into the water. He splashed his face, feeling stubble on his chin and deciding to leave it there until he reached Terlingua. The mist cleared and he felt the moisture drying on his face as he walked back to the fire with the metal hand once more in place.

Rosita Vasquez looked at him, smiling.

'Buenas Dias.' She held out a mug. 'Is it far to Terlingua?'

'A day.' Wyatt shrugged, taking the coffee. 'Not far.'

'You will write?' asked Rodrigo. 'You will not forget?'

'No.' She smiled at the *rurale*. 'I will write, Juan. Don't worry.'

Rodrigo grunted, then went over to his men.

'He is very possessive.' Wyatt wasn't sure if it was pride or promise in her voice. 'Sometimes he thinks he owns me.'

'Does he?' the American scooped a tortilla from the skillet sizzling on the flames.

'No one owns me.' Her dark eyes flashed, irritation showing momentarily through her smile. 'I am my own woman.'

'Where you headed?' he changed the subject.

'Albuquerque,' she said. 'My *tia* – my aunt – owns a rooming house there. Have you ever been to Albuquerque?'

'No.' Wyatt shook his head. 'I never seen it.'

'It is a big place.' She said it with total conviction. 'My aunt has often written, telling me what a great place it is. Juan would like me to stay in Villalta. He must, you see. He must do as he is ordered.'

'Man's gotta do what a man's gotta do,' Wyatt grunted through a mouthful of tortilla.

'That does not make sense,' she said, nibbling daintily.

'Does to me,' he retorted.

'But Juan would like to go to Mexico City.' She produced a handkerchief from her sleeve, dabbing at her mouth. Grease moistened her lips, emphasizing their fulness. 'But he is posted to Villalta. He must stay there until he is ordered somewhere else. So he cannot do what he would like to do.'

Wyatt shrugged. 'You want to go to Mexico City?'

'I want to go where there are people,' she replied. 'Where there are bright lights. Juan wants me to marry him. He would like me to stay in Villalta as his wife. He says it will not be long before he is sent somewhere else, but I do not want to wait.'

'You aimin' to come back?' Wyatt took a second tortilla from the pan. 'After Albuquerque?'

The woman's smile got wider, dark lashed lids folding over her big eyes in a conspiratorial expression.

'If I tell you something, you will swear it is a secret between us?'

Wyatt nodded: 'Sure.'

'I do not know.' Her voice dropped as she said it. 'My aunt writes that a girl like me – a girl with a voice like mine – could do well in Albuquerque. Perhaps I shall stay there.'

'Yeah.' Wyatt smiled back at her. 'A girl like you could make plenty in Albuquerque.'

'But perhaps I will go somewhere else,' she murmured. 'Who knows? I may come back. If Juan is sent to Mexico City. Or I may go to California. Or St Louis. Do you know those towns?'

'No.' Wyatt shook his head. 'I been to Houston. Saw San Antonio once. Mostly, I been in a place called Black Rock.'

'Is that where it happened?'

She looked at the metal hand. It was impossible to tell whether it was sympathy or curiosity he could hear. He nodded and said: 'Yeah. That's where it happened.'

His tone halted her next question, the smile fading slowly from her lips. She wiped them again and stood up, brushing at the creases in her skirt.

'I must prepare to leave,' she said, eyes expressionless.

'You do that,' Wyatt said. 'Soon as you're ready, we'll pull out.'

He finished his tortilla and drank the last of the last coffee. The sun was warm on his back as he went over to the tether line and threw his saddle on the bay stallion.

Rodrigo came to join him.

'You will be there by nightfall?'

'I guess.' Wyatt nodded, stooping to draw the cinch tight. The stallion swallowed air and he drove a knee into the animal's belly, hauling on the strap as it snorted. 'Before dark, I'd reckon.'

'Good.' The Mexican's face was thoughtful, as though he found himself for once at a loss for words. 'You were talking with Rosita . . .'

'Yeah.' Wyatt chose to settle the man's doubts: there was no point to making an enemy of the captain. 'She was tellin' me about her aunt in Albuquerque. Said she's staying in her rooming house. Said you want a posting to Mexico City.'

Rodrigo smiled, reassured. 'That is right. I have already applied. When I get word, I shall send for Rosita. Then we shall be married.'

'That's nice.' Wyatt began to fasten the bridle. 'I hope you're both happy.'

'We shall be.' Rodrigo said it with confidence, but Wyatt could hear the doubt lurking behind the assurance. 'It is only a matter of time.'

'Yeah.' Wyatt came close to feeling sorry for the man. Not quite close enough to telling him exactly what Rosita had said. 'I guess that's how it is.'

Rodrigo nodded. 'You will guard her.'

It wasn't a question, and Wyatt felt the twinge of sympathy disappear. He nodded back; curtly.

'Like I told you.'

'Good.' Rodrigo paced beside him as he walked the bay over to the phaeton. 'I thank you for this.'

Wyatt hitched the stallion behind the wagon and climbed onto the drive seat. Rodrigo put his arms around the woman and kissed her full on the lips. She responded briefly, then pulled away, waiting for the Mexican to hand her up. She settled on the seat beside Wyatt and he caught the waft of scent, heady in the still morning air. She arranged the folds of her skirt demurely about her legs and smiled down at Rodrigo. He said:

'Vaya con Dios, querida.'

She pouted a kiss in his direction and Wyatt nodded goodbye. Rodrigo lifted a hand in salute and farewell as the big American flicked the reins and sent the phaeton lurching forwards over the sand. The horses splashed into the water, spray rainbowing from their passage. Behind, the bay stallion snickered and quickened its pace, slackening the halter line. The river was shallow, rising no higher than the animal's fetlocks, the bed firm, not slowing the wagon. Wyatt steered directly over, rolling out on the far side with the sun slanting down on his right. Rodrigo stood watching them, waving as Rosita twisted in the seat, the movement pressing her body close against Wyatt, to lift a hand in reply. Wyatt didn't look back.

The river faded into the heat haze behind them. Ahead, the terrain stretched out flat and yellow, broken by the stark thrust of saguarro and the bluish-grey mottling of chaparral. Buzzards spun circles in the sky above, black specks against the blue. Off in the undergrowth a bird trilled out a series of shrill notes then fell silent. The Mexican highlands were a misty bulk to their rear, dark against the brilliance of the sky. The air was getting steadily warmer, no breeze lessening the mounting heat. Rosita fluttered a hand before her face, coughing lady-like in the dust raised by the horses. She looked sideways at Wyatt from under downcast lashes, smiling as she said:

'Now we are alone.'

'Yeah,' Wyatt grunted.

'I am in your hands.' She went on smiling as she touched the metal appendage resting on his thigh. 'Forgive me – your hand.'

Chapter Five

The sun was an incandescent globe, so brilliant it was impossible to define against the silver-blue of the sky. Shadow pooled in tight circles about the feet of the saguarros, the big cactus plants shining green and spikey in the noonday heat. Wyatt brought the phaeton to a halt where a stand of algarroba afforded a degree of shade and climbed down. Rosita Vasquez took his extended hand, her palm dry, and followed him onto the ground.

'Such heat.' She began to fiddle with the buttons of the nip-waisted jacket she wore. 'It is cooler in the hills.'

'You get used to it.' He used his stetson to water the animals, grateful for the cool dampness as he set the hat back over his thick, brown hair.

'Only if you have to.' She removed the jacket, exposing the thin cotton blouse beneath. 'I do not intend to.'

The blouse was fitted tight, thrust out by the swell of her breasts. Sweat had darkened it, plastering the material sheer against the contours of her body. Wyatt saw that beneath it she wore only a fine camisole, her breasts clearly delineated. He wondered if it was the heat that prompted her to remove the jacket, or the desire she had shown to flirt with him. She was an attractive woman, that was undeniable. But he felt nothing towards her: it was as yet too soon after Josie's death. He passed her the canteen, watching dispassionately as she drank, the backwards tilt of her head jutting her bosom harder against the near-transparent material.

'I shall live in a hacienda,' she continued, returning the canteen. 'Like a real lady. It will be cool and there will be servants. I shall not get used to this.'

Her gesture encompassed the desert country, the heat,

the dusty phaeton. Wyatt shrugged, swilling tepid water about his mouth. It was possible, he thought. Equally possible that she would wind up in a whorehouse someplace. It made no difference to him: she was a merely a step along his path to Vance Jennings and the others. He wondered where Jennings was now – whether the outlaw was still waiting at the Tres Pinos crossing, or heading back for Terlingua. It made little difference: by nightfall he would reach the town; see the woman safely into a hotel and continue his hunt. He corked the canteen and hunkered down with his back against the gnarled trunk of an algarroba.

Rosita glanced at him, her eyes thoughtful for a moment, then – as though reaching some decision – she settled beside him, legs thrust out to expose her ankles. The scent she wore was heady on the hot air, a bedroom smell that, by force of contrast, reminded him of the clean freshness of Josie, the scent of her hair, the honey-sweetness of her body. And the memory set his features in hard lines, the planes of his face grim as he stared moodily at the gleaming metal of his left hand.

'Does it hurt?' Rosita's voice was husky in his ear. He could not tell if she spoke of his missing hand, or the memories etched on his face.

He chose to believe it was the hand and shook his head: 'No. Not now.'

She opened her mouth to speak again, but when she saw his face she let the words die unspoken in her throat. Wyatt closed his eyes, pushing the memories away.

The shadows were beginning to elongate as he climbed to his feet. The woman followed him and they started off again, moving due north through the burning afternoon. The land folded in a series of shallow corrugations, the trail winding over the ridges and down into the troughs. Wyatt held the team to a steady pace, a billowing cloud of dust marking their passage across the arid landscape.

The heat continued unabated, no cloud showing in the unmarred blueness of the sky, heat haze shimmering off the ground in flickering waves that made distance hard to judge.

They were rolling towards the crest of a ridge slightly higher than the other gentle folds when the left side pony baulked. Wyatt grunted, yelling at the horse as it snickered nervously, falling out of step with its companion.

And then the sand ahead erupted upwards. Rosita screamed. The nervous pony reared, the right side animal joining it.

A shape exploded from the sand. A dust-covered blanket flapped back as a black-haired figure sprang upright, sun striking bright off metal. Wyatt saw long hair flutter beneath a scarlet headband, a dirty shirt, muscular legs under a loincloth. Then the brightness of the metal was lost in the neck of the left side horse. The animal screamed, crimson jetting from its throat. It began to buck, legs tangling in the harness so that as it went down, it brought the second animal with it.

The big man acted on pure instinct. His left arm thrust out, slamming against the woman. She was clutching at his wrist and the sudden movement of his arm spilled her clear of the phaeton to sprawl full length on the sand. Wyatt let go the reins, right hand dropping to his holster. His fingers closed on the warm butt of the Colt, thumb snapping the hammer back as the pistol cleared leather. The gun lifted, flame spouting from the muzzle as it lined on the Apache.

The Indian's mouth was open in a fierce whoop of triumph, blood from the dying horse sliming his features. Then there was only redness. Wyatt's bullet struck the bridge of the hooked nose, just below the eyes. A hole appeared, bone showing briefly white before a cascade of red hid detail as the .45 calibre slug ploughed into the skull. The eyes crossed, turning inwards under the impact, dragged back into the gap where the face had been to dissolve in pulpy ruin as the bullet entered the interior of the head. The Apache's upper lip curled in what looked like a snarl, drawn taut by the implosion of his features. Black hair plumed about the bullet's exit passage and a thick column of blood that was filled with shards of broken bone and sticky, grey brain matter fountained over the earth. The Indian danced backwards, arms extended as though he prayed, then one moccasined foot snagged on chaparral and he thudded down.

Wyatt powered clear of the phaeton as war-cries replaced the thunder of the Colt. He saw three Indians coming in fast on horseback, heeling their mustangs up the far side of the ridge. Adrenalin flooded his nervous system and he saw as though in slow motion that two held horn bows, the third a Henry repeating rifle. The wagon stood between him and the woman, and he shouted at Rosita to run for the cover of the vehicle as he moved towards the bay stallion.

A feathered shaft imbedded in the side of the wagon, polished wood splintering under the stone tip. He heard a bullet from the Henry ricochet from an upright. And he slashed the claws of his metal hand through the line holding the stallion to the phaeton. As the big horse screamed, eyes rolling as its ears flattened back, he snatched the Winchester from the saddle boot, hooking his claws into the lever. The stallion reared, spinning in its own length and began to run back down the slope. Wyatt let it go, hurling himself for the rear of the phaeton as the three warriors went by in a wild charge.

Dust clouded his vision as he dove for the underside of the vehicle. When it cleared, he saw Rosita down on her belly beside him, the Apaches turning their mustangs for a second charge. An arrow ploughed sand a foot before his face and he thrust the Colt towards the woman.

'You know how to use it?'

She nodded, snatching the pistol from him. She

clutched the gun in both hands, using her left thumb to draw the hammer back.

'You got four shots,' he yelled over the thunder of the charging ponies. 'Don't waste them.'

He turned back to face the Indians. His left arm was extended forwards, the Winchester's barrel resting between the claws. He snatched the lever down, pumping a shell into the firing chamber. And the rifle bucked against his shoulder, filling the space below the wagon with the sharp reek of black powder.

A mustang screamed as the .44-40 calibre slug tore into its chest. It went down with crimson spraying over the warpaint, haunches lifting as it somersaulted in a great rolling cloud of blown sand. The rider was pitched forwards, his drawn bow driving an arrow deep into the earth. He twisted with feline agility, landing on his shoulder to come up on both knees with another shaft already notching against the gut string. Wyatt fired blind, spraying shots at the riders, traversing the Winchester directly across their approach. The unhorsed bowman loosed off one feathered shaft, the arrow spanging from the metal wheel rim on Wyatt's left. Then he grunted as crimson blossomed on his chest. The bow fell from his hand and a thick gout of scarlet gushed from his mouth, more from his nostrils. He put both hands on the ground, hair hanging long and lank about his face as he spat blood, the sand below his head becoming pooled with the stuff as his ruptured lung poured out a steady welling of bright scarlet.

Wyatt twisted, watching the remaining horses go by. Rosita triggered the Colt, her eyes wide and frightened, the pistol bucking in her two-handed grip. The hammer clicked dully on an empty chamber and Wyatt shouted for her to take fresh loads from his belt as he rolled to cover their exposed side.

The Apaches were swinging round, dividing to hit them from both sides at once. Wyatt felt the woman's hands tugging cartridges from the belt loops, and scrabbled round to angle the rifle at the Apache with the Henry.

Dust drifted on the still air, obscuring sight as the Indians closed again. Wyatt heard the Colt bark. Felt a bullet from the Henry tug at his hair. The Apache was coming in on a straight line as though determined to charge his pony head-on against the wagon. The American lifted his arm, angling the Winchester up. He squeezed the trigger. And the man on the horse was lifted from the pad saddle, the Henry blasting a shot into the sky. Wyatt's bullet took him in the belly, low down, angling up through the abdomen to exit above the pelvic girdle. The Apache rolled over the mustang's haunches and the animal swerved clear of the phaeton, thundering away into the chaparral. The Apache hit dirt and screamed as the fall drove jetting blood over his naked legs. He twisted, face contorted with pain, and drew a long, curve-bladed knife from his belt. Blood was running down his thighs as he lurched to his feet and staggered towards the phaeton. His lips were drawn back from his teeth in a feral snarl of rage and pain, left hand pressed against the hole in his abdomen as he raised the knife high above his head. Wyatt fired again. The bullet hit the Indian in the throat, tearing through the flesh on the right side to sever the pulmonary artery. A great arc of blood pumped from the wound and the warrior's head turned, eyes glazing in agony as his heart pumped life from the hole. He was dying as he moved forwards, body glistening redly as the outpourings of his punctured belly and neck drenched his shirt, soaked into his loincloth. Wyatt triggered a third shot. It landed between the ribs, bursting the heart so that a wash of dark blood erupted from the Apache's shirtfront, stark against the brighter flow. His knees buckled and he folded slowly, almost gracefully, onto the sand. His eyes stared sightlessly into Wyatt's, then he leant sideways, legs kicking straight as his blood-soaked hair touched earth.

Wyatt heard the woman scream and scrabbled round, the Winchester an encumbrance now, its barrel clattering against a wheel. Rosita was flat on her belly, the Colt pushed out to one side by the brown hand clutching her wrist. The remaining Apache was flat on the sand, left hand fastened about the woman's right wrist, the other seeking to thrust a Bowie knife into her throat. She was holding him off, her fingers slender about his knife hand, tendons stark along the underside of her arm.

Wyatt let go the Winchester and drove forwards, digging his boots into the earth as he sought purchase. His left hand stabbed out, reaching past the woman's head. The claws extending from the metal hand gouged into the Apache's face. Two hit the right eye, the third the left. Abruptly, the orbs were clouded with crimson, the razored metal slicing deep through cornea and pupil and lens. Wyatt felt the blades grate on bone and twisted his wrist, tearing deeper into the pulpy stuff of the vitreous humour. The Apache's scream echoed shriller than the woman's. He let go his hold on her wrist, body jerking in agony fierce enough that he tugged free of Wyatt's stabbing hand. The knife fell from his grasp as he rolled back, spine arching as he reached for the twin red holes in his face. Blood flowed in crimson gouts from the holes where his eyes had been and his mouth stretched back wide in a lung-searing shriek. Wyatt moved clear of the phaeton, left arm lifting as he straddled the screaming Indian. He brought it down and across in a swinging arc that slashed the claws over the warrior's throat. The skin parted in red lips that peeled back from the open gap of the windpipe. Air whistled from the cuts and the writhing of the man's body tossed Wyatt away. He came up on his feet as the Indian brought his hands down from his savaged eye sockets to the red maw where his throat had been. Crimson spilled over the sand, covering the Apache's hands, running thick down his wrists and forearms. The whistling sound died away to a choking and the hands fell loose, fingers digging into the earth, lifting the body in a final, spasmodic attempt to escape the pain. Then the choking became a moist rattle. Moccasined heels drummed against the sand and the warrior was abruptly limp, falling back, deflated in death.

Wyatt turned towards the lung-shot Indian. The man was flat on his face, down in a wide pool of blood that was already drying in the hot sun. Flies were buzzing about his head, crawling thirstily over the congealing crimson. His face was turned to the side, scarlet bubbles frothing from his wide open lips. Wyatt saw a fly settle on his cheek, walking delicately over the dark skin. He bent down, taking the Colt from Rosita's hand. The pistol was empty and he wedged the barrel between his claws to thumb the loading gate open and eject the spent shell casings. He reloaded all six chambers, then walked over to the dying Apache. The warrior seemed unaware of his presence as he cocked the Peacemaker and put the muzzle close to the head. He squeezed the trigger, flies darkening the air as the skull exploded.

He went back to the wagon, grey eyes scanning the terrain for sign of further attack. There was none, and he beckoned the woman out.

She was trembling, face pale beneath the tan as she stared at the carnage. Her lips moved silently, then she fell against him, arms clutching as though she feared the corpses might rise up to renew their onslaught. Wyatt held her, feeling her breasts against him, the shaking of her body.

'It's over,' he said. 'We're safe now.'

He felt tears dampen his shirt, but after a while her trembling eased and she moved away from him, not quite letting go her hold. He put his hands on her shoulders, looking down into eyes that were no longer seductive. Just big and very scared.

'We're safe,' he repeated. 'You're all right.'

She nodded, still not speaking. Then suddenly pulled

away from his grip, turning her back on him as she clutched at her stomach and bent over with vomit spilling from her mouth. Wyatt waited until the heaving ended, then passed her the canteen.

'Get cleaned up.' He smiled at her; reassuring. 'I have to go find my horse.'

He saw the bay stallion standing wary down in the trough. The reins were tangled in the branches of a mesquite, the horse shaking its head as it tried to pull free. He approached it slowly, crooning softly as he got closer and the ears flattened back, fear showing in the rolling eyes. He got the animal gentled down and brought it back to the phaeton. The stabbed horse was dead and he worked the harness clear of the corpse, setting the stallion in its place. Rosita was calmer, already on the drive seat. Not looking at the bodies. Wyatt cleaned the blood from his metal hand and reloaded the Winchester, setting the rifle on the boards at his feet.

'You saved my life.' She touched his arm as she said it, fingers tightening. 'I am in your debt.'

Wyatt shrugged. 'No problem,' he murmured, grinning. 'I done it hands down.'

Chapter Six

Night had fallen by the time they reached Terlingua, light sparkling through the darkness in promise of safety and rest. Wyatt took the phaeton down Main Street to the town's one hotel, halting outside the single-storey adobe building and helping the woman descend. He lifted her luggage from the rear and set it on the sidewalk as she stood watching him, her gaze nervous.

'What do I do with this?' he asked, pointing at the vehicle.

'Sell it.' She shrugged. 'I don't care.'

'I'll take it to the livery.' He picked up a trunk. 'But first, let's get you settled in.'

'Tyler?' It was the first time she had used his name. It sounded like a plea. 'Don't leave me alone here. *Por favor?*'

He looked at her. Suddenly she seemed vulnerable. He shrugged.

'All right. I won't. Not until the stage leaves.'

'Thank you.' Her voice was husky, but there was no hint of flirtation in it; just fear. '*Muchas gracias*.'

'De nada.' He kicked the door open and set the trunk down, turning back for the second. 'Don't worry.'

'I won't,' she said softly. 'Not while you're with me.'

The desk clerk looked up as they approached, an appreciative smile spreading over his sallow features as he took in the woman's figure. He smoothed back pomaded hair, the smile freezing on his face when he saw Wyatt's metal hand. He fiddled with the bulky knot of his greasy tie, covering his surprise behind a professional facade.

'Folks?' His voice was thin and high, adam's apple bobbing in his throat as he spoke. 'You lookin' for a room?'

'Two,' Wyatt said.

Rosita added, 'And a bath.'

'Sure.' The clerk looked from one to the other, trying not to show his curiosity. 'You want to sign the book?'

He opened a big, leather-bound register, the binding cracked and ink-stained, turning it towards them. The woman signed her name and Wyatt put down an indecipherable scrawl. The clerk blotted the signatures and fetched two keys down from the hooks behind him.

'You want a hand?' A flush suffused his face as he realized what he had said. 'I'm sorry, mister. With the trunks, I meant.'

'Forget it.' Wyatt picked up the keys. 'Yeah – send them along.'

He crossed the vestibule to the door at the rear, opening it onto a long, low-ceilinged corridor with a single window at the far end and doors opening off. The rooms were dirtier than in Villalta, the bare planks of the floor dusty, the narrow windows looking onto the saloon across the dividing alley smeared with grime. Each held a wooden bed with a chair on one side and a wash-stand on the other. One had a rickety-looking wardrobe, the second just a row of hooks. Wyatt saw Rosita settled in and went back to the vestibule.

'The Albuquerque stage?' he asked the clerk. 'When's it leave?'

'Your guess is as good as mine.' The man shrugged. 'You ain't heard?'

'Heard what?' Wyatt asked.

'We got injun trouble.' The clerk nodded sagely. 'Buck called Salvaje come off the Bosque Redondo on the prod. Got hisself a bunch of broncos an' headed this way. Army chased him to the border, then give up when he crossed. He's been raidin' outta Mexico since. Hit the stage last week. Bastard killed Marshal Coombes, too.'

Wyatt kept his face straight as he asked, 'That mean there ain't another?'

'Don't know fer sure.' The clerk spread his hands. 'Should be one through from El Paso in a coupla days. Won't know until it shows up.'

Wyatt nodded, grateful for the fact that the broncos were getting blamed for the killing of Rafe Coombes; mildly irritated that he couldn't get Rosita off his hands sooner.

'Where do I buy tickets?' he asked.

'Right here.' The clerk grinned, reaching under the desk to produce a folder of stage dockets. 'Ain't got no depot, so passengers get on here. How many you want?'

'One,' Wyatt said. 'To Albuquerque. Make it out for *Señorita* Rosita Vasquez. She'll pay you.'

'Yeah.' The clerk looked confused by the arrangements. 'She ain't with you?'

'She's her own woman.' Wyatt shook his head. 'I'm just seeing her through.'

'I wish,' the man started to say, then broke off when he saw the expression on Wyatt's face. 'Yessir! I'll get that done.'

'Thanks.' Wyatt went out the door onto the sidewalk. Light was shining from the saloons and he could hear a piano tinkling over the sound of voices. Across the street the frontage of the bank was lit by the glow, the bars covering the windows gleaming dully. He paused, staring past the phaeton at the square, flat slab of the building, a thought forming in his mind. Vance Jennings was known in Terlingua – he might have friends ready to back him against a solitary stranger. But if Wyatt could draw him out of the town . . .

The big man smiled to himself as he climbed onto the drive seat and lifted the horses to a walk down Main Street.

The marshal's office was dark, the door closed. Wyatt wondered if that meant there were no deputies, that Coombes hadn't been replaced yet. He went past the office and halted outside the livery. The same stablehand was there, mouth gaping as he saw Wyatt.

'Figgered you for dead.' He scratched vigorously at the wart on his cheek. 'Or runnin'.'

'Why'd I run?' Wyatt jumped to the ground.

'Well, hell.' The stablehand shrugged. 'Way you was askin' about Rafe Coombes, then him windin' up dead.'

'I heard Apaches got him.' Wyatt hauled his saddlebags from the wagon. 'Bronco called Salvaje.'

'They said it looked that way.' The stablehand's eyes moved from Wyatt's face to the metal hand. 'Said he was all cut up.'

'But you thought different,' Wyatt said.

The stablehand got a cunning look in his eyes. 'Man don't pay good money fer information less'n he aims to use it. You wanted word on anyone askin' about you. I give you that word. Got five dollars fer it. Then Rafe got killed. Put two an' two together an' it makes four.'

'Six,' Wyatt said, coldly.

'What?' The man frowned.

'Six deep by six long. A grave.'

As Wyatt said it he brought his left arm up. The blades set into the metal hand touched the ostler below the chin, pricking into the soft flesh of the underjaw. He started to step back, then realised the movement would slice the claws into his mouth. Wyatt raised his arm a little, lifting the man onto his toes.

'I'd say Salvaje done it,' he rasped. 'Were I you.'

The stablehand decided against nodding.

'Another thing.' Wyatt held the claws against the man's jaw. 'Anyone says different, I'll remember who told me about Coombes. Don't reckon folks'd like that too much.'

Sweat beaded the warty face as Wyatt lowered his arm. Shifty eyes glared at him with a mixture of fear and hatred.

'All right.' The ostler's voice was husky. 'You got a deal.'

'That's good,' Wyatt said. Now let's talk another. You seen Vance Jennings around?'

'No.' The man shook his head. 'Not since you was here last time. He come through, but he didn't stay over long. Don't know where he went.'

'He have anyone with him?' Wyatt cradled the metal hand in his right, light from the lantern hung over the doors reflecting off the metal.

'Three men.' The stablehand's gaze was transfixed by the claws. 'Big feller with a face looked like it got pushed through a meat grinder. Runty guy in an old cavalry suit. An' a fancy-lookin' dude with a funny accent.'

'Good.' Wyatt smiled and angled his left arm at the phaeton. 'You want to give me a deal on that? The horse, too.'

The man glanced at the wagon. He shook his head.

'That's Rafe Coombes' bay you got there, mister. I ain't buyin' no dead man's horse. Not the way Rafe got killed.'

Wyatt cursed his oversight. He had gotten used to the bay: he hadn't thought to change the animal when he had the chance.

'You got a point. Suppose you just stable him nice an' quiet? Where people won't see him.'

Greed overcame fear. The stablehand grinned: 'Cost you extra.'

'How much?'

'Two dollars?' The man scratched some more at his cheek. 'A day.'

'That's goddam robbery,' Wyatt complained.

'That's insurance,' the man shrugged. 'Like you said about folks not likin' things too much? Don't reckon they'd like some stranger ridin' Rafe's pony.'

Wyatt grimaced. 'All right. We got a deal. What about the wagon?'

The man went over to the phaeton, casting a professional glance over the vehicle.

'Looks like you met up with Salvaje.' He touched a broken arrow shaft. 'Guess you was lucky.'

'Guess I am.' Wyatt smiled again. 'Gives me a real good

reason for riding Coombes' stallion. Anyone spots him, you can tell them I found him running loose after the Apaches hit.'

'It's still two dollars a day,' grunted the stablehand. 'An' I'll give you twenty on the other pony. Fifty on the wagon.'

The phaeton was worth more, but Wyatt decided against arguing it. It wasn't his and the profit the man was making could seal his mouth tighter. He nodded.

'Wait there.' The man scurried into the stable. 'I'll get yore money.'

He came out with a wad of greasy notes in his hand, counting out the seventy dollars. Wyatt stuffed them into his pants and took his Winchester off the wagon. As he turned away the stablehand said:

'Mister? Next time you quit Terlingua, don't come back.'

Wyatt grinned, not answering as he walked back down the street towards the closest saloon. He checked them all, buying a single whiskey in each and taking his time drinking it as he studied the occupants. There was no sign of Jennings or the other two surviving outlaws, but he caught the mood of the town. It was frightened: the Apache raids had the citizens running scared.

He went back to the hotel and dumped his gear in his room. The promised tub was brought and he took a bath, then shaved the stubble from his jaw and changed into his last clean shirt. He was dressed when the woman knocked on his door.

She was changed into a black skirt and white blouse, her raven hair fastened back off her face with a comb.

'I got seventy dollars,' he told her.

She shrugged, not interested. '*Tengo hambre*. Let's eat.'

'Sure.' Wyatt took her arm and they headed for the dining room.

'Jesus Christ! The red bastards are everywhere.'

Vance Jennings passed a spy glass to Coltrane, gesturing at the terrain below their position. They were bellied down on the rim of a bluff, the scarp falling away fifty or sixty feet to the flatlands below. Over to the west, the sun was painting the sky a brilliant red, like the glow from a burning building. Shadows threw long over the ground, stretching out the saguarro in stark patterns against the yellow of the sand, the chaparral blue in the waning light.

Coltrane lifted the glass to his eyes and grunted.

Through the telescope he could see upwards of twenty Indians grouped about a big fire. There were more coming in from the canyon over to the east, and a file of around ten or fifteen moving in from the south.

'What the goddam hell's goin' on?' he wondered aloud. 'What's got them stirred up?'

'I ain't about to go ask them,' Jennings whispered, voice husked by the slash across his throat. 'But they're between us an' Terlingua.'

'Looks to be a war meeting.' Coltrane said, his own voice lowered as though he feared the Apaches would hear even over the distance between them. 'There must be around sixty down there.'

'It's a goddam army,' Jennings agreed. 'Maybe Jean run into them.'

'Wade an' Andy, too?' Coltrane murmured. 'Ain't too likely, Vance.'

'Could have happened.' Jennings went on staring down at the Indians. 'Them red heathens jumped reservation, they'd have the Army after them. Most likely, they'd run fer Mexico an' raid back across the border. Blue-bellies wouldn't follow them over the river.'

'Some would.' Coltrane went on staring through the spy glass, as though the panorama below fascinated him. 'Remember that crazy man, Dundee?'

'Yeah.' Jennings spat. 'I remember that silver, too.'

Coltrane folded the glass and passed it back. He looked nervously at the thin-faced man.

'You really think they got Jean?' he asked. 'All three?'

'Christ, Simon!' Jennings shook his head, his confidence

shaken. 'I don't know. I know they never showed an' I know the silver never showed. Past that I ain't got no more idea than you.'

'What we gonna do?' Coltrane eased back from the rim. 'We could ride back south.'

He said it hopefully, wanting Jennings to agree. Wanting to get up on his horse and run for the safety of Mexico.

Jennings looked across the flat to where the terrain broke up in long, mesquite-dotted folds. His eyes were hard; angry. Things had gone wrong since that raid on Black Rock and he was starting to get a feeling that luck was no longer running his way. Maybe they should have taken the proceeds of the raid and lit out some place other than Terlingua, but that had seemed the obvious thing then: the town was safe and Rafe Coombes had gotten word to him that it was a good time to go ahead with the plan they had discussed so often. The Mexicans trusted Coombes and his word had been that the silver amounted to their biggest shipment yet. It had been too much for Jennings to resist: with Cole Garrett dead, one big hit could have set him up. Got him off the outlaw trail with enough money to cover his tracks. But now? Now he didn't know where the hell Andy Chance and Wade Martin were. Or Jean DuPré. They should have come back to the Tres Pinos ford when it was obvious the silver shipment was being sent by another route. Andy and Wade, left alone, might have gone on waiting, but the Creole was too smart for that. He would have guessed something had gone wrong and come back fast. So where the hell was he? Unless Coltrane was right, and they had been jumped by the broncos.

But somehow that didn't seem right to Jennings. He had an ugly feeling there was some other reason. And he didn't want to think about it.

'No.' He shook his head. 'There ain't nothin' there for us. Our money's in Terlingua.'

'An' them hostiles are between us an' there,' said Coltrane. 'So what we gonna do?'

'Wait up some more.' Jennings fingered the bandanna covering his throat. 'A day. Maybe two. They ain't gone by then, we'll ride around them. We're goin' back to Terlingua an' get our money.'

He eased clear of the rim and slithered down to where Strother Cannon was holding the horses. The scar-faced man looked at him with a question in his eyes.

'There's goddam injuns crawlin' all over,' Jennings husked. 'We can't go through them, an' it's gonna be close on two days if we ride around them. We'll wait up here a spell.'

Cannon nodded and took the horses over to where a ravine cut through the bluff. He stripped off the saddles and tethered the animals inside the shelter of the split. Then he set to gathering brush wood, taking care to choose only dry timber that would show little or no smoke. He did it with unquestioning patience: Vance was the boss.

'I feel better.'

Rosita dabbed a ladylike napkin over her lips and filled their coffee cups.

'You still have to wait for the stage,' Wyatt reminded. 'If it comes through.'

'No matter.' She sipped coffee, smiling at him over the rim of the cup. 'So long as you are here.'

Wyatt frowned. The idea that had formed since he saw the bank didn't take into account the fact that he might wait up in Terlingua. But somehow he didn't feel ready to leave the woman. It wasn't anything sexual: Josie's memory was too close for that, too fresh in his mind. But that same memory made him loath to quit on Rosita – she seemed to place the same kind of trust in him that Josie had. And that trust had faltered once: he didn't want to see the same kind of look in another woman's eyes.

'You will stay?' Rosita leant forwards to touch his hand. 'Please?'

'Sure.' He nodded with less reluctance than he felt. 'I'll stay.'

'Thank you.' She smiled at him. 'I do not feel safe here.'

Wyatt followed her gaze around the room and understood what she meant. The place was only partly filled, but apart from two women in bright red dresses that matched the garish shade of their lips, the other diners were all men. They had been watching Rosita throughout the meal, their obvious interest outweighing the fascination of Wyatt's metal hand. Left alone, he guessed she wouldn't last long before someone – or several – dragged her off into a room. Just like Josie. He smiled back.

'Don't worry,' he murmured. 'You'll be safe.'

She nodded. 'So long as you are here. I trust you, Tyler.'

Trust. The word cut like a knife. I don't want trust, he thought. Not again. I don't want anyone tying me down. I want to find Jennings and Coltrane and Cannon. I want to kill them. And you could get in the way. Don't trust me.

'I'm beat,' he said. 'You ready to sleep?'

She nodded again, a hint of her earlier flirtatiousness returning. She rose to her feet and he followed her from the dining room, down the corridor. She paused at the door of her room, toying with the key.

'You can come in,' she whispered. 'If you like.'

'No.' Wyatt shook his head. 'I ain't ready for that. Not yet.'

She saw the pain on his face and said, 'I could help you forget.'

'I don't want to forget,' he replied.

'A man's gotta do what a man's gotta do?' She parodied the words he had spoken back at the river.

'Something like that,' he said. 'And right now – forgive me – you're not it.'

Chapter Seven

Two days went by slowly. There was no further sign of Indian activity, but the air of anticipation Wyatt had sensed continued to linger in the town. No riders came in, and none went out. Men passed the time in the saloons, or lounging on the sidewalks, the chief topic of discussion Salvaje's break-out. Rumours abounded: Salvaje was gathering the biggest raiding party the territory had seen; the broncos had crossed the border, running deep into Mexico; the Army had surprised the Apaches and wiped them out; the Apaches had jumped a pursuing column of troops and wiped out the Army. Wyatt listened, keeping himself to himself and his eyes open for sign of Jennings. He got worried that the outlaws had run into the broncos, fearing that the Apaches had beaten him to his revenge. But there was little he could do: Terlingua was his only real lead to Jennings and the others, so he had to sit it out. Inaction was hard to bear.

Then, soon after noon on the second day, the stage showed. It was escorted by a column of cavalry, commanded by a lieutenant. The troopers rode in with tired faces, uniforms colourless under a coating of dust. A crowd gathered as the concord drew to a halt and the lieutenant ordered his men to dismount. He climbed onto the sidewalk, raising his arms for silence.

'Name's Tyree,' he announced. 'Lieutenant Tyree, United States Cavalry. I come up from Fort Quitman. I guess you folks are worried about the hostiles.'

A man in the crowd called, 'Goddam right we are, bluebelly.'

Tyree grinned. 'There's sign south of here, and east.

Looks like Salvaje's got around a hundred renegades. They hit a ranch close by Latigo.'

Another voice said, 'Christ! That ain't but three days' ride away.'

'Looks like they've gone over the river,' Tyree continued. 'Way the sign looks, they took the ranch an' run some cows over into Mexico. Most likely, they'll stay down there a spell.'

'You can't be sure of that,' someone called. 'What you gonna do about it?'

'We're patrolling the border.' Tyree slapped dust from his pants, blue emerging from the coating of grey. 'They come back over, we'll be waiting for them.'

Wyatt looked at the fifteen troopers standing patiently in the street and wondered what the lieutenant hoped to accomplish against a hundred hostile Apache warriors.

'I run into some,' he said, 'three days ago. Due south of here.'

The officer looked at him, blue eyes meeting grey.

'Where were you coming from?'

'Villalta,' Wyatt answered. 'Over the border.'

Tyree nodded. 'Most likely some bucks going down to join Salvaje. Or stragglers. There been any other sign?'

'Not lately.' It was the hotel desk clerk who spoke. 'But the marshal was killed a while back.'

'Yeah,' a voice agreed. 'They cut him to pieces.'

'Well,' Tyree put a reassuring smile on his youthful face. 'Reckon you're safe enough now. It's not likely they'd chance hitting a town. Not like this.'

'What about the stage?' asked the clerk. 'What happens with that?'

'Up to the driver.' Tyree looked to where a grizzled man in a long, yellow duster stood watching. 'My orders were to ride escort this far, no farther.'

'Ben?' The clerk looked at the driver. 'What you gonna do?'

Ben shrugged, directing a thick stream of tobacco juice

with neat precision at a cockroach scuttling busily over the sidewalk, then glanced at his guard. The shotgun rider was younger, around Wyatt's age, with lazy eyes set in a vacant face. He canted his scattergun over his shoulder and said, 'Up to you, Ben.'

'All right.' Ben pulled off heavy gloves. 'We pull out soon as we got the horses changed. Army says them renegades are south o' here, we got a fair chance to make a clear run. But I ain't hangin' around givin' Salvaje time to double back. We leave in one hour. Anyone's comin' with us, they better be ready.'

He took a wad of tobacco from his coat and carved off a chunk, popping it into his mouth as he turned for the saloon. The guard followed him and the crowd began to break up. Tyree beckoned a sergeant forwards.

'Kincannon? Get the horses watered. The men can stand down for an hour. Then we ride.'

The sergeant looked old enough to be the officer's father. He touched a hand to the brim of his battered campaign hat and drawled a casual 'Yessir'. Wyatt headed for the saloon.

The driver and the guard were up at the bar drinking whiskey. Wyatt pushed through the crowd to stand beside them.

'You be going through Black Rock,' he asked.

'Sure.' Ben nodded. 'All the way through to Albuquerque.'

'There'll be a man in the Belle,' Wyatt said. 'Doc Mortimer. Will you give him a message?'

Ben nodded again. 'So long as it ain't so long I can't remember it.'

'Tell him Tyler Wyatt's coming back,' said the big man.

Ben repeated the words twice, like a child reciting a lesson.

'Sure,' he grunted. 'I'll do that.'

'Thanks,' Wyatt said. 'I appreciate it. Tell him your drinks are on me.'

He turned away, going out of the saloon back to the hotel. He knocked on the door of Rosita's room and when it opened, he told her of the impending departure. She looked at him with a mixture of anticipation and regret in her big, dark eyes.

'You won't be coming with me?'

'I still got business to attend,' he murmured. 'You'll be safe enough.'

She nodded. Then: 'I must get ready.'

'I'll see you off,' he smiled.

Before she could say anything more he went into his own room and gathered his gear. He settled his bill at the desk and walked down Main Street to the livery. The stablehand took his money and led him down to the far end of the stable, where the light was dimmest and the bay stallion was penned inside a stall draped round with sacking. Wyatt saddled the horse and brought it out to the front. The street was empty, but he decided against taking the chance of someone recognizing Coombes' horse and rode the pony down an alley emerging at the rear of the livery. He put his heels against the flanks and took the big animal around Terlingua in a wide-swinging circle that brought him back to the west side of the settlement, facing the rear of the bank.

The building was a flat slab of adobe, the wall facing him devoid of windows, flanked on either side by stores so that he dismounted unnoticed and left the horse tethered amongst some mesquite growing close to the blank wall. On foot, he ambled casually down the gap between bank and store, then along the sidewalk at the front to glance down the second alley. There was a single window on one side that he guessed fed light to the manager's office, none on the other. The front held a big, solid-looking door sided by two windows with thick bars over the glass. The door stood open, and when he looked in, he saw a wide room with the tellers' cages set midway down, steel grillwork reaching from desktops to ceiling in an unbroken division. There was a door off to the right with the word *Manager* lettered on a teak plaque. Three tellers stood behind the grill and there was no sign of a guard.

Wyatt was smiling as he crossed Main Street to the hotel.

Rosita was waiting in the vestibule, wearing the green travelling dress. Her two trunks were on the sidewalk.

'Will I see you again?' she asked. 'I'd like that.'

'Maybe.' He shrugged. 'Maybe I'll come through Albuquerque some day.'

'I will be with my aunt.' She smiled up at him. 'Tia Juanita's, her place is called. She writes that it is the finest rooming house in town.'

Wyatt nodded, hearing the stage brake to a halt outside.

'I'll remember that.' He took her arm. 'Tia Juanita's.'

He felt a vague reluctance as he handed her onto the concord, a regret at leaving her. The thud of the closing door put some kind of full stop to whatever might have happened between them. An episode was ending, and he doubted that he would ever see her again – and that, in a way he could not define, saddened him. She would go on to Albuquerque and he would continue his lonely hunt for the killers of his wife. He should have felt relief: her going took a responsibility he had not welcomed from him, left him free – unhampered – to hunt down Jennings and the others. Yet he was sorry to see her go.

He raised a hand as Ben yelled at the horses and the stage rolled into movement. The woman's face showed at the window, staring back at him with an expression that seemed to mirror his own feelings. He heard her call, '*Vaya con Dios*, Tyler,' and then she pulled back inside as dust clouded from the team's hoofs, rolling down Main Street as the concord gathered speed.

Wyatt waited until it was out of sight, turning as he heard Lieutenant Tyree bellow an order and the column of troopers cantered past, heading south. He watched the cavalry disappear into the heat haze, lounging back against the frontage of the hotel as he waited for the street to empty. It was mid-afternoon now, the air hot and still. The dust settled slowly, drifting lazy over the sidewalk, undisturbed by wind or movement. Wyatt walked over to the bank.

The room was cooler than the street, the thick adobe walls holding out the heat, the windows not letting in too much light. The floor was stone, heavy slabs set directly onto earth and morticed to form a smooth, hard surface. Wyatt's boots rang on the stone as he crossed to the nearest teller. The man looked up from the column of figures he was adding with an expectant smile on his face.

'I need to talk with the manager,' Wyatt said. 'It's urgent.'

'Mister Tyson?' The clerk set a ruler across his columns. 'I'll see.'

He went down the far side of the cage and unlocked a door. The counter swung open and he ducked beneath the grillwork to tap on the door with the plaque. A muffled voice told him to enter and he went inside. Wyatt stood by the door, waiting. It opened and the clerk came out.

'Go right in.' He looked like he didn't believe Wyatt had much to talk about. 'Mister Tyson's waiting.'

The big man stepped through the door and shut it behind him. He was in a small room, partitioned off from the main part of the bank by a thick wood wall. It was even cooler than the outer area, fancy Mexican tiles covering the floor, a big map of the Southwest Territories on the wall behind an ornate desk. The desk was set at an angle in one corner so that light from the single window fell across the glistening mahogany surface, shining on the bald head of the man seated in the big, leather-stuffed chair. He was a small man, his eyes coming level with Wyatt's shoulder as he stood up. They were small, dark blue eyes set in a round face that seemed disproportionately large for the features. Tyson's nose was small and snubbed and reminiscent of a pig's snout, his mouth a thin-lipped gap above several chins that folded over the collar of a spotless white shirt with a pale green tie at the neck. He wore an expensive-looking grey suit, a gold watch chain spanning the protuberance of his vested belly.

He set small hands with chubby fingers on the desktop as he said, 'I understand you have urgent business to discuss, Mister . . .?'

Wyatt heard the question mark at the end of the sentence and said, 'Tyler Wyatt.'

Tyson gestured at a straight-back chair set facing the desk.

'Sit down, Mister Wyatt. How can I help you?'

Wyatt sat, good hand and metal hand resting on his thighs. Tyson stared at the metal hand and frowned. Wyatt grinned, offering no explanation.

'I come from Black Rock,' he said. 'You know the place?'

Tyson shook his head. Wyatt went on grinning, looking past the little man at the big safe on his right. It reached halfway up the wall, a brass dial on the front with numbers from one to twenty around the rim, a plate with the legend, *Bailey & Duane, Chicago, Ill*, set below the dial.

'Vance Jennings deposits money here,' he said.

'Mister Jennings is a client.' Tyson's voice was prim. 'Did he recommend my bank?'

'Why I'm here,' Wyatt answered.

'Ah.' Tyson sounded reassured. 'Mister Jennings perhaps told you of our – how shall I put it? – special arrangements.'

'No questions?' Wyatt said.

'It is not our business,' Tyson sounded prim again, 'to query the nature of deposits. We accept money on good faith, and we do not disclose the source or any details of our clients.'

Wyatt nodded. 'It don't matter where it comes from.'

'Not our business,' said Tyson. 'Do you wish to avail yourself of our services?'

Wyatt guessed that he was asking if he had money to deposit and shook his head.

'No. It's more like a withdrawal.'

Tyson frowned again. 'I don't quite understand. Did Mister Jennings send you? If so, I shall require a note. Identification of some kind.'

'Jennings would know me.' Wyatt lifted his metal hand. 'By this.'

The banker's face got nervous. His fingers drummed briefly on the desk, then tucked into the pockets of his vest. Wyatt watched as they moved on down, out of sight below the mahogany. Tyson leant forwards.

'I think,' he said, 'that you had better explain why you're wasting my time.'

'I'm not,' Wyatt replied. And came out of the chair as the banker pulled back with his right hand coming out of a drawer holding a little Remington over-and-under.

His thumb was pulling on the hammer as Wyatt hurled himself across the desk. He felt the rim hit his legs, swinging him forwards as his arms reached out for Tyson. His right hand clapped over the man's mouth, fingers digging viciously deep into the loose flesh, pinching off the cry of alarm. His left drove down onto Tyson's, smashing the fingers wide and flat so that they sprang loose from the derringer. The blades of the metal hand went through the soft skin. Wyatt heard them grate on bone. Felt them imbed in the mahogany beneath. The banker's cyes opened very wide, white showing around the dark blue. His florid face got pale as a muffled scream tried to escape around Wyatt's grip. The big man lifted his left arm, turning his wrist so that the movement brought Tyson's hand with it.

The blades jutted from the banker's palm, crimsoned where they had pierced flesh. Red ran in three thin trickles over the skin. Onto the immaculate white of the shirt cuff. The Remington remained on the desk.

Wyatt got his feet on the floor and eased around the desk, pulling Tyson closer towards him. He kept his wrist turning, twisting the banker's hand so that the claws dug hard against the delicate bones. Tyson whimpered. A dark stain spread across the front of his grey pants.

'You make a sound an' I'll kill you. You understand?'

Tyson's head was gripped too hard for him to nod: his eyes gave the answer. Wyatt let go his face and drew the Colt. The Peacemaker's hammer clicked loud as it went back on full cock. Wyatt pressed the muzzle against the spreading flab of the banker's belly. Tyson swallowed, sweat beading his porcine features. His lips trembled, mouth hanging open as his eyes turned to stare in horrified amazement at his pinioned hand.

Wyatt kept it thrust out as he said: 'Jennings took upwards of three thousand dollars out of Black Rock. How much you got here?'

'Exactly three thousand.' The banker's voice was a high-pitched quaver. 'Oh, my God! My hand!'

'I can do worse,' grated Wyatt. 'Where you got it? In the safe?'

Tyson nodded.

'Good.' Wyatt's grin was feral. 'I'm gonna take it. You got a kerchief?'

Amazement showed in the banker's eyes, but he reached down, warily drawing a square of dark silk from his pants.

'Ball it up,' Wyatt said. 'An' then stuff it in your mouth.'

Tyson obeyed. And Wyatt yanked his left arm back. The blades came free of the pinned hand in a splatter of red. Tyson's groan was dulled by the gag, his eyes staring horrified at the crimson spreading over his palm, the back of his hand. He clutched at the wounds, blood running between his fingers to spoil the front of his vest, dripping down to stain the already-soiled front of his pants. Wyatt kept the Colt hard against his belly, shoving the fat little man backwards until he was jammed against the safe.

'Open it,' he ordered. 'Don't try anything.'

He eased the Peacemaker back, waiting until Tyson was down on his knees, left hand pressed against his vest as he fumbled with the combination lock. He put the Colt against the back of the bald skull as tumblers fell into place and the heavy metal door swung open. The banker fetched out a satchel with *Jennings* stencilled on the canvas. Wyatt hooked claws into the material and swung the bag round, onto the desk. Tyson began to reach for more satchels, but Wyatt shook his head.

'No. That's all I want. Stand up.'

Tyson climbed laboriously to his feet, nostrils dilated as he struggled to breathe through the blockage of the gag.

'Spit it out,' Wyatt said. 'Then count the money.'

The banker spat the kerchief onto the floor and began to fumble with the strap fastening the satchel. It was difficult: the fingers of his right hand were stuck out stiff where bones had broken. He got the satchel open and began to count the notes inside one-handed. Wyatt eased the hammer of the Colt down and holstered the pistol. He picked up the Remington, levelling the stubby barrel on Tyson's chest.

'It's all there.' The banker started to replace the notes, staining them with red. 'Oh, Jesus Christ! Please don't kill me.'

'No.' Wyatt's voice was cold as his eyes. 'You've got a message to give Jennings. When he comes back, you tell him I killed Andy Chance. Wade Martin, too. An' The Creole. Jean DuPré. You got that?'

Tears showed in Tyson's eyes as he nodded, joining the sweat running down his plump cheeks, dripping salty onto the blood pooling over the desktop.

'Tell him I took the money he stole,' Wyatt added. 'Tell him that Tyler Wyatt took it. Back to Black Rock. I'll be waiting for him there.'

Tyson nodded again, his voice low as he said, 'I'll tell him. He'll kill you.'

Wyatt went on grinning. It looked more like a snarl. He hooked the claws into the banker's vest and stuffed the satchel inside his shirt as he pulled Tyson across the office to the window. There was a trail of blood spots over the tiles. He eased the window open and tossed the Remington out.

'Tell him he's got one more deposit to make,' he rasped. 'Himself. In a grave.'

Then he swung his left arm up and round. The lower part of his metal hand slammed against Tyson's neck, where jaw and skull met. The banker's eyes glazed and he began to slump. Wyatt hit him again, the solid part of the metal hand landing against the temple. Tyson went down in a small, round heap.

Wyatt climbed through the window and ran for his horse.

Chapter Eight

Vance Jennings stared at Tyson with pure contempt in his eyes. The banker made an ostentatious display of the bandage wrapping his hand, glancing nervously at the three men crowded into the office. Lamplight did nothing to soften their hard features, seeming rather to emphasize the hideous scars decorating Strother Cannon's face, the shifty, gun-happy eyes of Simon Coltrane. Mostly it seemed to focus Jennings' rage, settling his lean face into hard planes rendered somehow more menacing by the whispery voice.

'You mean we rode through half the goddam Apache nation fer nothin'?'

Jennings fingered the bandanna covering the scar on his neck like a hangman testing the knot on a rope. Tyson swallowed and said:

'For God's sake, Vance, what could I do? He put that metal through my hand. He held a gun on me.'

'You could've hollered,' Jennings suggested harshly. 'You could've raised a posse.'

'Here?' Tyson shrugged elaborately. 'You really think that would have got you your money back?'

Jennings didn't answer. Just went on staring at the banker as though he contemplated which way to kill him. Tyson felt his shirt get sweaty on his back and eased his ample buttocks to a more comfortable position on the big chair.

'Why don't we just take three thousand?' Coltrane suggested. 'Don't make no difference where it comes from.'

Jennings shook his head, his contempt transferred for a

moment to the slump-shouldered man in the ancient cavalry uniform.

'Christ! I gotta deal with fools all the time?'

Coltrane flushed, face confused. 'What's wrong with that?'

'Tell him.' Jennings speared the banker with a furious glare. 'You got the brains to see it, don't you?'

'I think so.' Tyson nodded, thankful that the outlaw's anger was momentarily shifted onto someone else. 'What Vance is saying is that you aren't the only – uh – clients with this arrangement.'

'What I'm saying,' Jennings cut in, 'is that this fat bastard takes money off'n just about every owlhooter in the territory. We lift three thousand, it's gonna come outta some other feller's pocket. What'd you do if that happened, Simon?'

'It did,' Coltrane mumbled. 'I don't know.'

'Goddam it!' Jennings slammed a fist onto the desk, jumping an inkpot open so that long streamers of black liquid coursed over the mahogany, reminding Tyson of the way his blood had looked, running out of his hand. 'It means they'd come after us. You want a feud, Simon? You want fellers like us on yore tail?'

Coltrane shook his head, lapsing into silence.

'So Wyatt put us on a spot.' The name came spitting from the dark-haired man's mouth like a curse. 'The bastard knew it. Knew he wasn't leavin' us no choice except to go after him. He's countin' on it.'

'Will you?' asked Tyson.

Jennings' lips settled into a narrow line, tugging down through the greying stubble covering his chin.

'You can bet yore overfed ass we will, banker. I ain't lettin' no goddam blacksmith get the better of me.'

'He said he'd be waiting for you,' Tyson warned. 'In Black Rock.'

'I heard it,' husked the outlaw. 'An' that's where we're goin'.'

'Black Rock?' Coltrane's mouth gaped open, shock overcoming his fear of Jennings. 'That's crazy, Vance. They know us there.'

'What the hell else you suggest?' Jennings pushed a hand through his grey-streaked black hair. 'Ain't no money around here. Not with that goddam renegade Apache out on the prod. We can't lift Tyson's money without gettin' ourselves into a shootin' war with every other road agent in the territory, an' the stages ain't runnin' while Salvaje's out.'

'One did.' Tyson played the ace he had been holding back, seeking to curry favour. 'Wyatt put a woman on it.'

'What?' Jennings sounded surprised. 'What you talkin' about?'

'He came in with a Mexican woman,' said Tyson. 'I checked over to the hotel. Charley Brandon told me Wyatt came here with a woman called Rosita Vasquez. Said they looked real friendly. Then the stage came through from El Paso with a cavalry escort and Wyatt put the woman on board. Charley said she was going to Albuquerque.'

'When?' Jennings barked.

'Yesterday,' said Tyson. 'Around three.'

'Christ Jesus!' Jennings' voice got hoarser as anger mounted. 'Whyn't you tell me before?'

Tyson shrugged, not answering.

'All right.' Jennings made a visible effort to keep his whispery voice calm. 'Let me get this straight. Wyatt took our money an' told you he'd killed DuPré an' the others. Said he'd be waitin' for us in Black Rock. But before that, he put this woman on the stage for Albuquerque.'

'That's right,' Tyson said, touching the ugly bruise on his temple. 'That's exactly it.'

'An' they was close,' Jennings said. 'That right?'

Tyson nodded, wincing as the motion sent lances of pain throbbing through his skull.

'Didn't take him long to find hisself another woman,' Coltrane snickered.

'Won't take us long to catch up with the stage,' Jennings said.

'What for?' Coltrane asked, frowning. 'I thought we was goin' to Black Rock.'

'We are.' Jennings got on his feet. 'After. First, we're gonna catch up with that stage an' take the woman off. Wyatt was that close to her, she'll give us an edge.'

Strother Cannon made a sound for the first time since they had entered Tyson's office. It was a strangled moan; inarticulate, wordless. He moved his fingers in parody of running legs, then shook his head, aping exhaustion.

Jennings nodded. 'Yeah, I know. Our horses are beat. So we buy fresh mounts.'

'We ain't got no money,' said Coltrane.

'No,' Jennings agreed. 'But Tyson here does. He'll pay for them.'

Tyson looked at the outlaw's face and didn't argue. 'She's a day and a half ahead,' he warned.

'No matter.' Jennings moved for the door. 'Stage ain't gonna be travellin' by night. Not with hostiles around. We'll make up the time easy.'

He pulled the door open, looking back as Strother Cannon pointed a finger at Tyson, then at the door. When the banker hesitated, the scar-faced man grabbed a handful of coat and propelled him across the room. Jennings held the door open as Cannon put a foot against Tyson's rump and kicked him through, humour showing for the first time on his face as he saw the fat man's discomfort.

They went out of the darkened bank and walked their tired horses down the street to the livery. The wart-faced stablehand came out, looking warily at the three outlaws, curiously at the banker.

'Three ponies,' Jennings said. 'Runners. Fetch them.'

The stablehand paused, then ducked inside the livery as Jennings' hand touched the butt of the Colt holstered on his waist. He came out with three fresh mounts, not speaking as they slung their saddles on the animals.

'Tyson'll pay you.' Jennings swung astride a rangey buckskin. 'He's got an interest.'

He laughed as he slammed his heels against the horse's flanks, lifting it to a fast canter that took him out of Terlingua on a northeasterly line, following the stage route. Behind him, Tyson reached inside his coat for money, grateful to see his back.

Wyatt reined in outside of Black Rock. Off in the distance, its outlines blurred by the heat haze shimmering off the flatlands, the mesa that had given the settlement its name rose up dark against the blue morning sky. Beyond, the town sprawled sleepy in the sun: one more New Mexico town, with nothing about it to show the fury that had once consumed it. He swung down from the bay stallion, looping the reins about the gnarled limb of a wind-stunted liveoak and went on foot to where marker stones and wooden crosses jutted from the arid soil. He paused, looking down at two graves, the earth still relatively fresh. The sun had already bleached the paint on the two simple white crucifixes, cracking it and peeling it so that in places the words were obscured. He stooped down, flaking paint to expose the names again. One read simply, *Josie Wyatt*; the other, *Cole Garrett*. A few wilted flowers stood in a simple urn on his wife's grave. On her father's, the vase was overturned, the flowers scattered.

He looked at the markers for a long time, face set in an expression of pain. Then he turned away, going back to the horse and climbing onto the saddle, walking the animal slowly forwards to where the memories waited.

It was early, smoke from breakfast-heated stoves lifting leisurely into the sky. He saw the smithy, the cabin he had built behind, its windows shuttered, the door closed. In the roofed-over smithy, the furnace was cold and dead, the tools he remembered still racked neatly in their places. Outside Wilbur Meacham's store, the same brindle dog was spread across the sidewalk chewing on a bone; up at the farther end of the single street, the chapel stood, its white paint no longer fresh. It was all as he remembered it: the same; and at the same time, different because he was different. Black Rock had been his home. He had built a life here, but now that life was over and he was changed.

He reined in outside the Belle, hitching the bay stallion to the rail.

Inside, the saloon was cool and silent. Glasses stood on the long bar, covered neatly with fresh cloths. The floor was swept, chairs upturned on tables. It felt familiar and horribly strange. He went over to the bar, dropping the satchel containing the money on the polished wood, then reached over to take a bottle and pulled a glass from under the cloths. He felt like he needed a drink. He tugged the cork and spilled whiskey into the glass, drinking it fast as the memories threatened pain. He could see the support pillars where Vance Jennings had strung Cole Garrett, and his eyes moved instinctively to the floor, seeking sign of bloodstains. There were none, and his eyes moved round to where he had sat, lashed to a chair as the outlaws raped Josie. He filled the glass again and tossed it down, the liquor hot and anaesthetic.

And a whiskey-hoarse voice grumbled, 'What the hell you think you're doing? We ain't open yet.'

He turned, looking down the room to what used to be the door of Cole Garrett's quarters. A short, stocky man stood there, feet bare under crumpled pants, braces spanning a collarless shirt. His sandy-coloured hair was awry, the natural curls emphasized by the tanglings of sleep, the good-natured face screwed up in a frown.

'Drinking whiskey,' Wyatt said. 'That all right with you, Doc?'

'Tyler?' There was a note of disbelief in Doc Mortimer's voice. 'Is that you?'

'Sure.' Wyatt grinned as the doctor came shuffling down the saloon. 'How are you?'

'Tyler!' Mortimer's crumpled face split in a broad smile. 'My God! It's good to see you again.'

He halted in front of the larger man, eyes moving up and down Wyatt's muscular frame with professional appraisal.

'You lost weight. How's the hand?'

Wyatt turned the metal hand, still smiling. 'Fine. I got used to it.'

'No pain?' Mortimer fetched himself a glass, filling it to the brim. 'The stump healed?'

'Yeah.' Wyatt nodded, feeling pleasure for the first time. 'It handles real good.'

He tapped it on the satchel. 'There's three thousand dollars in there. All I could get back.'

Mortimer glanced at the satchel. Back at Wyatt, seeing the coldness behind the smile. He topped his glass.

'You caught up with them?'

'Three,' Wyatt said. 'Wade Martin, Andy Chance an' DuPré. They're dead.'

Mortimer's eyes followed his glance to the metal hand and he didn't ask how. Instead, he said: 'The others?'

'I took their money,' Wyatt murmured. 'I left word where I'd be.'

'Here?' There was shock in the doctor's voice now. 'They won't risk coming back here.' Then, nervously: 'Will they?'

'I think they will.' Wyatt's smile was no longer pleasant. 'They was fixing to hit a silver train on the border. I stopped that. The way I got it worked out, they don't have no money. An' three of them are dead. Jennings will want me for that.'

'When?' Mortimer set his glass down. 'We'll be waiting for them.'

'No.' Wyatt shook his head. 'It's between me an' them, Doc. They're mine.'

'You're crazy.' The older man touched Wyatt's sleeve.

'We can get ready for them. Shoot them down like dogs.'

'No!' Anger tinged the big man's voice. 'I do this alone. I want them to know who's killing them. I want to see their faces.'

'Tyler.' Doc Mortimer shook his head, looking suddenly older, tired. 'You've changed.'

'They changed me.' Wyatt emptied his glass and set it down. 'You want to give me some breakfast? Then we'd best take this money to Abner.'

Abner Teech managed the Black Rock stage depot. With Doc Mortimer and Wilbur Meacham, he was one of the three men who knew that Wyatt had gone to Terlingua after the outlaws.

'Sure.' Mortimer shrugged. 'Come on back. I moved into Cole's old rooms – seemed like if I was running this place for you, that made more sense.'

Wyatt nodded: Cole Garrett's only living kin had been Josie, and when they both died the saloon had become his. He had no interest in it, so had entrusted its running to Doc Mortimer.

'I got the books,' said the doctor as they went into the rooms at the back. 'You want to see them?'

'I trust you.' Wyatt shook his head. 'I'll take some money when I move on.'

'You're not staying?' Mortimer asked. 'When it's done?'

'I don't think so.' Wyatt sat down in a chair he remembered. 'There's nothing for me here. Not anymore.'

'There's a home,' said Mortimer. 'Any time you want it.'

'I had a home,' Wyatt grunted, not bothering to explain more.

Mortimer nodded and began to break eggs into a pan.

'When d'you think they'll get here?'

Wyatt shrugged. 'I don't know. Most likely, they'll come fast. Jennings must be pretty mad at me.'

'For what you did?' The doctor added bacon. 'I guess they must be.'

'Yeah.' Wyatt smiled again as he stared at the metal gleaming on the end of his left arm. 'They must be pretty cut up.'

Chapter Nine

Rosita Vasquez stared at the arid landscape rolling past the concord's window. It stretched out in a yellow panorama hazed by heat and the dust rolling from the pounding hoofs of the six horses stretching out under the yells of the driver. Saguarros stood like giant grave markers in the sand; cholla and chaparral seemed as arid and hostile as the blinding sun or the silvery, cloudless sky.

She pressed a scented handkerchief to her nose and thought about Albuquerque as she tried to ignore the weight of the man seated to her left. His name was Anson; he was a drummer. A sample case was clutched upon his knees. It held – he had shown her the contents; proudly – an assortment of gewgaws he hoped to peddle around the frontier towns. She had looked at the cheap glass jewelry and turned up her nose. When she got to Albuquerque she would buy the real thing, not coloured baubles. Anson had seen her contempt and given up trying to impress her. Now he dozed, multiple chins folded onto the frontage of his canary-yellow vest, grey-sleeved arms locked over his precious case. Beyond him, a thin man dressed all in black stared from the window on his side with a bored expression on his smooth-shaven, handsome face. He had ignored the drummer's eulogy, smiling at Rosita over the greasy black hair of the enthusiastic peddler. He was called Tevis McQuade and he was travelling all the way through to Albuquerque, where he owned an undertaking parlour.

Facing McQuade was a ruddy-faced man with silver-grey hair and a slow Texas drawl. He called Rosita *Señorita*, and spoke to her in slow Spanish. His name was Walter Haskins and he was a cattle buyer for an Eastern stock company. He was getting off at Black Rock. Next to him was a rancher called Ethan Ford. He had occupied Haskins – when the stock buyer wasn't speaking to the woman – with a fulsome description of the quality of EF brand cattle. Haskins had casually agreed to make Walker Springs his next stop after Black Rock and take up Ford's invitation to look over the cattle. Their conversation had fascinated the younger man crushed between the window and Ford's bulky shoulder. His name was Andrew Garvin. He was twenty-two years old; from Macon, Georgia, where he had worked in a hardware store. His family had been killed during the War, when Sherman led the march through Georgia, and three months ago his uncle Jonathan Garvin had died childless and left Andrew four thousand dollars and a ranch in Wyoming. The earnest young man had chosen to travel west by the longer stage route, rather than use the faster means of rail and river transport, because he wanted to see the Real West – he put capitals on the words – like uncle Jonathan had written him. His enthusiasm got boring after a while, but Rosita kept smiling at him and pretended to share it: four thousand was a lot of dollars.

Of the five men in the sweat-pungent coach only three carried visible weapons. Walter Haskins wore a Remington's Army model in .44 calibre in a flapped holster around his lean waist. Ford had a Colt's Peacemaker slung butt forwards on his left hip. Andrew carried a pair of Smith & Wesson Schofields – good enough for Frank James, so good enough for anyone – in new-looking holsters tied down on either hip.

Rosita wondered idly why she had felt safer with Tyler Wyatt than with these three well-armed men. And told herself to forget him. He was gone; she'd not see him again. Why should she want to, anyway?

She breathed in the scent from her handkerchief and wished for the next way-station. There wouldn't be a bath, but at least there would be fresh water to take the dust off her face.

'Simon! You take the horse. Strother, get the guard. I'll take the driver.'

Jennings bellowed the words over the thunder of the galloping horses. Ahead, a plume of drifting dust marked the stage. It was running fast, making good time over the flatlands; but not so fast that the three fresh horses couldn't overtake.

'Guard's gonna spot us,' Coltrane yelled back. 'He'll be firin'.'

'Scattergun off a runnin' coach?' Jennings' croaking whisper was contemptuous. 'We gone up against worse.'

'From the front'd be better.' Coltrane meant *safer*. 'We could go past. Swing round an' get ahead by night.'

'Too long.' Jennings shook his head. 'I want the woman now. Sooner we take her, the sooner we reach Black Rock.'

Coltrane nodded, not willing to take the argument further. He went on drumming his heels against the piebald's ribs, flattening closer against the neck as he matched Jennings' buckskin's long-legged stride. That way he made a smaller target: Vance was right about the scattergun. And if it was the kind of cut-down job most guards favoured, it wouldn't carry more than a few yards. And the guard would be firing over to the right where Strother would be. It should be all right.

The three outlaws ran shoulder-to-shoulder, using the faster ground of the hard-packed trail to make time.

They came up inside carbine range of the stage before they were spotted. The slack-faced guard eased round, peering back over the luggage piled on top of the concord's flat roof and shouted something to the driver. The coach picked up speed. Jennings swung his Winchester round to gouge the foresight over the buckskin's rump, the sudden pain spurring the horse to a wild-eyed burst that took it up alongside the rocking body of the stage. Coltrane saw Strother Cannon swing over onto the looser ground flanking the trail, the big LeMat shotgun-pistol looking normal-sized in his giant hand. Then Coltrane whooped and heeled his own pony faster as he put Jennings between himself and the driver as he overtook, lifting his own Winchester to his shoulder as he angled the muzzle in towards the left-side leader.

Smoke blew past his face as he went through the discharge of his own shot. He saw blood splatter over the neck of the lead pony, coming in a thin spurt from the hole at the base of the animal's skull. More coloured the froth streaming from the right-side horse's nostrils as the bullet emerged. The head shot horse dropped as though it hit a wall. Its legs folded like limp rags, the body crashing onto the dirt, tangling the harness so that the companion animal was hauled over to add to the barrier into which the rest of the team crashed.

Coltrane swung wide and out, turning the piebald in time to see the driver lift from the seat, propelled by the .44-40 slug blowing a great chunk of crimsoned flesh from his back and hauled by the reins looped around his left wrist. His mouth was open in what was either a scream or an automatic reaction to the shock of the bullet. Either way, the sound was lost along with his face as he went down under the hoofs and the piling bodies. One pony stamped metal-shod hoofs all over his skull and then he was crushed between the wheelers.

Over on the far side Strother Cannon had seen the guard's two-barrel swing in his direction and gone down along his horse's neck. The shot that peppered the animal's rump had only served to swiften its pace so that the second barrel blew ten gauge through empty air. Cannon had come back into the saddle with the LeMat pointed up close to the guard's ribs. His scarred face was split by a twisted smile as he squeezed the trigger and felt the blast of the eighteen bore load kick back against his hand. The guard's blue shirt was suddenly red. Bone showed jagged-edged in the hole, glistening internal organs swelling and tearing against the shards. Crimson exploded through the dust cloud, droplets gleaming in the sunlight as the guard was hurled sideways across the drive seat. His arms flung up, tossing the emptied shotgun away into the chaparral. He crashed down, bouncing off the seat as the concord piled into the fallen horses to arc through the air, a loose-limbed, bloody ragdoll that thudded limply onto the sand and lay there, bleeding.

The stage piled into the dropped team and crashed to a halt. The three outlaws faced the doors, Jennings and Coltrane replacing their Winchesters with handguns. Cannon snapped the hammer lever of the LeMat to revolver fire.

A man's head appeared through the left-side rear window. It was a handsome head, thick black hair falling over wide-set blue eyes that crossed and crashed inwards as Jennings fired. A woman screamed as the rear of the skull blew away, spraying the interior of the coach with blood and pieces of brain. Then the door flung open and a tall man with a Remington's Army model in his right hand hurtled through. He got off one shot before Coltrane and Jennings triggered bullets into his chest, slamming him back against the stage so that he fell backwards onto the floor, crimson pulsing from the holes in his chest as his eyes stared sightlessly into the raw hole that had been Tevis McQuade's face.

Andrew Garvin pushed clear of Rosita's lap and shouted, 'Best get down, miss.' Unnecessarily: she was already on the floor. He hauled both Smith & Wessons out of the holsters and kicked the right-side door open. Strother Cannon fired the LeMat into his belly as he powered out. The .42 calibre slug tore into his gut, doubling him over in mid-air so that the Smith & Wessons blew holes in the dirt. He was still twisting as the scar-faced man fired again, blasting a bullet into his back. It broke the spine, deflected by its impact with the column of bone to glance off into the heart. The youngster was dead before he touched ground.

Ethan Ford put both hands in the air and shouted, 'Don't kill me, boys! I'm comin' out slow.'

He got as far as the door before Cannon shot him in the chest, smashing him back over Rosita's body with huge spurts of dark blood fountaining from the wound. It drenched the woman's hair, running hot and slick over her face, salty on her tongue as she opened her mouth wide and screamed.

Jennings came down off his horse, running forwards to thrust his Peacemaker into the coach. He saw Haskins and McQuade tangled up on the floor, not moving. The woman struggling to push clear of Ford's body. And Armstrong Anson of Shreveport, Louisiana, holding on to his case of samples with his eyes screwed tight shut and his lips trembling. Jennings shot him in the head, adding to the crimson already painted over the inside of the concord.

A horse screamed in pain, the sound cut off by the thunder of Coltrane's gun. Then there was silence.

Jennings' voice was a crow croak, dry as the scorched-powder smell of the air.

'Come out, lady.'

Rosita wriggled from under Ethan Ford's corpse and clambered over the two bodies blocking the door. She saw a thin-featured man with a red bandanna wound high about his throat pointing a Colt at her, his hawkish face creased with an ugly smile. Beyond him there was a fair-haired man in a faded cavalry uniform, watery eyes alight with lust as he stared at her. She gasped as the third man rode around the concord, yellow teeth showing in a sneering smile that rendered the hideously disfigured features even uglier.

Jennings put out a hand, grabbing her dress and yanking her clear of the coach. She sprawled on the sand at his feet, tears filling her eyes as his whispery voice said:

'Guess you'd be Rosita Vasquez?'

'I have no money.' She stumbled over the English. 'I have nothing.'

'Don't look like that from here.'

Coltrane snickered, licking his lips as he peered at the disarray of her garments. She tugged her skirt down over her thighs, feeling the material slimy with blood and pieces of brain.

Jennings said: 'Forget it, Simon. We ain't got time. Not now.'

Rosita got on her knees, face level with Jennings' hips. She shook her head, repeating over and over again the single word, 'Please.'

'You was with Tyler Wyatt,' husked Jennings. 'Back in Terlingua.'

It was a statement, not a question, and she remained still, arms folded over her breasts as she waited for the man to speak again.

'You was close, I heard. How close?'

When she still failed to speak, Jennings curled hair about his left hand and jerked her brutally to her feet. His right came up, palm landing hard against her cheek. Her head rocked sideways, scalp agonized as he tugged her abundant hair taut. Fresh tears burst from her eyes as he backhanded her, slamming her teeth together so that she nipped her lip, the smaller pain somehow lancing through the ache of her head.

'He fuck you?' Coltrane tittered.

'No.' The words came out through trembling lips. 'He helped me. He brought me over the border.'

Interest flickered in Jennings' black eyes. 'From where?' he asked.

'Villalta.' She wished she was back there. Safe with Juan. 'In the hills.'

'I know where it is.' Jennings let go her hair. Somehow his not touching her was worse than the blows. 'Christ! It all makes a goddam pattern.'

He turned to Coltrane as Cannon began to strip the corpses of valuables.

'You see it? The bastard musta jumped Rafe Coombes. Musta gotten Rafe to tell him where Andy an' Wade were holed up. He musta jumped them an' then taken Jean. That's why they never showed. Christ! He musta even got word to the greasers. Why they stopped the silver goin' by the Tres Pinos crossing.'

His words broke through the paralysis terror had locked on Rosita.

'I am engaged to Juan Rodrigo,' she said; formally. 'He is the captain of the Villalta *rurales*. He is a very important man, who will hunt you down and kill you like dogs if you harm me.'

Jennings husked laughter and said: 'He's on the wrong side of the border, lady. An' right now, he's most likely fightin' off a bunch o' hostile Apaches. Me, I'm right here an' now. Ain't no goddam greaser gonna come ridin' to yore rescue. It only happens like that in the dime novels.'

She clutched at a fresh straw: 'Tyler Wyatt will kill you.'

The name wiped the smile from the outlaw's face, thin lips curling in a snarl. He took hold of her dress, buttons popping down the front, and began to slap her rhythmically. Pain sparked bright lights across her eyes. She felt her mouth cut on her teeth. Felt one tooth bang loose, a lance of stabbing agony driving through the numbness spreading like hot ice over her cheeks. Blood ran down her chin, mingling with the mucus streamers dribbling from her flared nostrils. A ringing filled her ears. Like the funeral tolling of the church bell back in Villalta. It became a peel that dinned inside her skull until it was as though a gigantic clapper smashed against the walls of her mind, roaring out a sound that turned the world to red.

It was worse when he stopped. The pounding went on, but now it was joined by the fire burning up her face. The ache of the lost tooth was lost under the fierce torment consuming her cheeks. She was not aware that she lay on the sand, blood and spittle dripping from her mouth, her shoulders heaving as she sobbed.

Jennings dragged her to her feet again, the pressure on her scalp unnoticed.

'Tyler Wyatt's waitin' for me in Black Rock,' Jennings snarled. 'Only he ain't expectin' you along.'

'Like Find the Lady,' giggled Coltrane. 'We got her first.'

'Yeah.' Jennings nodded, glaring wild into her face. 'Now tell me about him. I left that bastard blacksmith one-handed.'

'He has metal.' She lifted her arm, fingers shaping into claws. 'A hand. There are three blades on it. Like the claws of a *tigre*. In Villalta, they called him *El Garra*.'

'What the hell's that mean?' Jennings asked.

'Claw,' she said. '*El Garra* means the Claw.'

Chapter Ten

'You get my message?'

Wyatt lounged back in the chair, long legs stretched over the floor of Abner Teech's office. The depot manager stroked his bald skull, half-frame spectacles glinting on his large nose as he shook his head.

'Ain't heard a word from nor about you, Tyler. Not since you rode out.'

The big man frowned, looking to where Doc Mortimer filled out a chair. The doctor's round face was blank as he imitated Teech's gesture.

'Maybe you beat the stage?' he suggested. 'Man on horseback would travel faster, anyway. And if there's Indian trouble, the coach could be slowed.'

'I guess.' Wyatt shrugged. 'Was only to say I was coming in.'

'It's late.' Teech sounded worried. 'Shoulda been through two days ago.'

Wyatt felt a prickle of concern; and wondered why. Rosita Vasquez wasn't anything to him. If she had run into trouble, it was her worry. He had his own.

'Leastways you got your money back,' he said.

Teech nodded. 'That's real good news, Tyler. Them outlaws ain't.'

'I told him,' Mortimer said, 'that we'll back him. There's not a man in town wouldn't hold a gun on those killers.'

'They'd be shot to pieces.' Teech nodded enthusiastically. 'Like mad dogs.'

Wyatt's metal hand rang on the chair's arm. The two men froze, staring at him. Slowly, eyes cold as grey ice on a winter stream, he looked from one to the other. His voice matched his gaze. It reminded Mortimer of a cold blue norther blowing over graves.

'They owe me,' he said. 'All they took from you was money. I got as much of that back as I could. You owe me for that. They owe me for Josie an' for Cole. An' for this.'

He lifted the metal hand, turning it so that the steel reflected the sunlight coming in through the window over their faces, mesmeric.

'I took three of them with this. I want the others the same way. So they know what they done to me. Why I'm killing them.'

Abner Teech's face went pale. He swallowed hard, taking the pince-nez off his hooky nose and polishing them furiously. Doc Mortimer shook his head like a man mourning the death of a friend.

'Tyler,' he said softly, sadness in his voice. 'You're turning killer.'

Wyatt's face was expressionless as he nodded.

'They made me that way, doc. Now they get the benefits.'

'God!' Mortimer shook his head slowly; resignedly. 'God help you, Tyler.'

'I'll help myself,' he grated. 'I don't want anyone butting in.'

'You alone?' Concern was in the doctor's voice now. 'Going up against three killers?'

Wyatt grinned. There was no humour in the expression, only a cold, deadly certainty.

'No,' he said. 'It won't be like that.'

'How's that?' Teech looked up from his industrious polishing. Fixed the half-frames back in place. Blinked. 'You brought them here. That's how you planned it.'

'Sure.' Wyatt went on smiling. Like a puma savouring a kill. 'But they won't ride in like before. They're known. They'll figure that out – Jennings ain't stupid. I figure he'll send word in somehow. Try to pull me out to someplace he feels safe.'

'Then what?' Mortimer's frown got deeper, cutting into the wrinkles already decorating his homely face. 'It'll still be one against three.'

'I know the country,' Wyatt said. 'This time I'm expecting them. The way I got it figured, I got thc upper hand.'

'Now what do we do?'

Simon Coltrane shifted his gaze from the heat shrouded shape of Black Rock to Rosita Vasquez. The way he looked at her gave his question a secondary meaning. Or maybe it was first in the outlaw's mind. The woman shuddered as Vance Jennings lowered his spy glass, voice whispering through clenched teeth.

'Not the woman, Simon. Not yet. That's for afterwards. We take Wyatt first.'

'How?' Coltrane asked. 'We ride in there, they'll blow us away. They ain't likely to have forgotten us yet a piece.'

'No.' Jennings' features were corded tight, hard lines stretching down from his nostrils, straining his neck above the bandanna. There was an insane light in his eyes. 'They'll remember us. So we ain't ridin' in the way he expects. We're gonna send him a message.'

Rosita shivered as his eyes locked with hers. Cold fingers dug icy nails into her spine as a warm knot curdled in her belly.

'It's gonna say that if he don't ride out alone, he gets his ladyfriend back one piece at a time. Maybe we'll send an ear – like a kinda guarantee.'

'Damaged goods?' Coltrane was thinking about the promised *afterwards*. 'He gonna want her back all cut about?'

Laughter whistled through Jennings' teeth like lost hopes.

'He won't let it go that far,' he said. 'Not the goddam blacksmith.'

'He killed the others,' murmured Coltrane. 'An' Rafe Coombes. Look what he done to Tyson.'

'Yeah.' Jennings nodded. 'Look what he done to Tyson. He stuck the fat bastard's hand when he coulda killed him. He only took our money when he coulda taken all of it. He coulda layed up for us in back of Tres Pinos, but he brought the woman up to Terlingua. Know what that means, Simon?'

Coltrane shook his head. Strother Cannon shrilled laughter, nodding enthusiastically.

'Means he's soft,' husked Jennings. 'Means he ain't gonna stand by while we butcher his ladyfriend. He'll come out, all right. Like a goddam lamb to the slaughter.'

'An' we lay up fer him?' Coltrane began to smile: it was looking easier. 'Backshoot him?'

'I want to see his face.' Jennings shook his head. 'I want him hung up like his goddam wife's old man. Like Cole Garrett was, Simon. I want to see Wyatt's face while I cut him.'

He touched the hilt of the cut-down sabre, stroking it gently; lovingly.

'So we gotta take him alive?' Doubt echoed in Coltrane's voice. 'That mightn't be easy, Vance.'

'We pick the place.' Jennings' hand closed around the sabre. His knuckles got white. 'Today, we scout out a spot. I'll hold the girl there. You two gonna be layin' up along the way.'

Coltrane didn't argue. Not with the crazy look in Vance's eyes. Instead, he asked:

'How we gonna get word to him, Vance? We ain't got but the three ponies. An' they're all wore out.'

'Ain't far to Black Rock.' Jennings went on gripping the sabre. 'An' we don't need but the one horse. We put the message on the saddle an' run it into town.'

'Christ!' Coltrane felt fear knot ugly in his stomach. 'You gotta get close to do that. You'd be spotted ridin' out.'

'You ain't ridin' out.' Coltrane heard the slight emphasis Jennings put on the *you* and felt the knot expand.

'You're gonna go in come dark. Ain't no one gonna see you then. Come dawn, you send the horse in. Put fire on its tail. Then you belly down an' wait for Wyatt to show.'

'Jesus!' Coltrane's voice was shrill now with fear, trembling on the verge of open revolt. 'That means I gotta be inside rifle range. On my own?'

Jennings nodded, eyes fixing Coltrane's, the madness in them dousing the embers of revolt. 'For a spell. Strother'll be farther down with his horse an' mine. You're gonna come up behind Wyatt an' shoot his animal. Remember that, Simon! Just the horse. Not him!' He paused until Coltrane nodded. Then: 'Strother'll come up at the gallop. You put guns on the blacksmith an' lay a barrel along his head. Get him trussed an' put him on a horse. Then you ride double back to where I'll be waitin' to collect. Me an' the woman, Simon. You remember that.'

Coltrane nodded again. The offer of the woman didn't quite compensate for the danger. But it was something.

'An' one more thing, Simon?' Jennings let go the sabre to grasp the front of Coltrane's tunic. 'You try to run out on me – you don't do it just like I say – I'm gonna kill you.'

Coltrane swallowed dryness. There was sweat on his face, misting his eyes so that they blurred more watery than ever.

'Like you say, Vance,' he quavered. 'I'll remember.'

'You better.' Jennings turned to Strother Cannon. 'You understand all that, Strother?'

The mute nodded eagerly, hands pantomiming knives hacking at his body.

'Yeah.' The awful smile on Jennings' face got wider, stretching his skin taut. Like a death mask. 'He cut himself in on more action than he can handle. Now I'm gonna cut him out.'

Chapter Eleven

A solitary buzzard drifted black against the burning sky. Heat haze, shimmering off the sun-bleached sand, hid Black Rock behind translucent waves that obscured the buildings, transforming the tall saguarro to trembling shapes like ghosts between the riders and the town. Ahead, a great dark sentinel standing black out of the arid prairie, was the mesa that had given the settlement its name. The sun stood behind and south of the rock, so that one part of it was bathed in brilliance, shining off the stone to render the darkness of the surface with a sparkling golden light. Where the sun did not strike, the rock was sombre, forbidding, featureless in the shadow and its own natural darkness. A great swathe of shadow fell over the arid land where the mesa blocked out the incandescent globe, like a patch of night cast ominous over the brightness of the day.

A trail worn hard over the sand showed where the inhabitants of the settlement had visited the rock. No fresh tracks showed on the trail; there were no marks, no horse droppings, no sign to indicate that the mesa was still a popular place to go. It was as though the settlement had got founded and paid its homage to the great dark buttress and then left it alone, slumbering blackly in the New Mexico sun.

Either side of the trail the terrain was flat. It stretched out in a panorama broken only by the bulk of the mesa. Cholla and chaparral patched the sand with dusty green, and stands of mesquite stretched twisted limbs low above the cactus growth. Saguarro grew in solitary splendour, spiney arms up-curved high over the smaller growths colouring the yellow streaks of sand. Simon Coltrane stared at the landscape and wondered where he was going to hide. The cholla was too thick to penetrate and the chaparral was tangled up too close to the ground. The mesquite would make good cover, but it was mostly growing too far back from the trail to allow for a certain shot. And he wanted to be very certain he'd hit Wyatt's horse: he didn't doubt that Vance would do just what he'd promised if the shot hit the wrong target. Which didn't leave Coltrane much choice apart from the old Apache trick with a sand-covered blanket.

The fair-haired man shook his head as he thought about it. He'd need to find a stretch of sand close to the trail. Get dug in and wait there, listening for Wyatt's horse. Then he'd need to time it exactly right. The hoofbeats would tell him how fast the horse was travelling, but he'd still need to be careful. If he shot Wyatt, Vance would carry out his promise. But if Wyatt got off the shot horse, he could be firing back. And he'd taken Wade Martin, who was a whole lot faster than Coltrane. And he'd taken Andy Chance, who was a whole lot stronger. And he'd taken Jean DuPré, who was tricky enough to be very careful. Coltrane didn't like the idea of going up against Wyatt alone.

He hoped Strother wouldn't waste any time getting up with the two horses. In air this still, the sound of a rifleshot would carry clear to Black Rock, which could mean a whole bunch of townsfolk riding out to see what was happening. But the mute would have to lay up some distance farther out to keep the animals hidden, so there would almost certainly be a period when Coltrane was alone with Wyatt. Hell! he decided. Goddamit if he'd get himself shot taking the bastard alive. If Wyatt came off that horse with a gun in his hand, Coltrane would try for a leg shot. Bring him down and hope to pistol-whip him before he got a chance to try anything. But if that didn't work, then he'd kill the blacksmith and take a chance with Vance.

He spat, feeling like he'd been given a choice between a knife in the belly and a bullet in the back.

Ahead, Strother Cannon was matching Jennings' canter, slumped hard and heavy in the saddle. His huge shoulders stretched the material of his sweat-stained shirt taut, the cotton threatening to split under the pressure of his muscles. He rode hatless, the dead, scarred skin that marked his scalping seemingly impervious to the heat. It glistened under a coating of sweat, a lifeless, yellowish corpse-colour. Coltran wished it was the mute taking the forward position: he was crazy enough to enjoy it. Which was probably why Vance hadn't picked him. In a fight, Strother could go wild: just kill Wyatt and forget anything Vance had said.

So it came right back to Coltrane, and there wasn't a single damn' thing he could do about it.

Alongside Cannon, Jennings was riding tall in the saddle. He sat the buckskin like a man going somewhere and eager to arrive, his back straight so that his stance reminded Coltrane of a captain he'd once served under. He'd been crazy too. Tried to lead a charge against a rebel artillery battery at Waynesboro that was obviously suicidal. Would have done it, too, if Coltrane hadn't put a .44 calibre ball in his back. He'd sat his mount just like Vance was now. And he'd gotten a wild light in his eyes when he wanted something bad enough to kill other people getting it.

The woman was seated behind Jennings with her arms wrapped tight around his ribs. Coltrane thought about those breasts pressed against his back, and felt a little better. If it all went well, they'd get to her before long. He rubbed at his crotch, remembering how she'd looked when she'd washed the blood from her hair and her body. She hadn't known he was watching, but he could see those tempting breasts as clear in his mind as they'd been then. He began to smile at the thought.

They got closer to the mesa, dwarfed beneath its size, and Jennings slowed.

They circled the rock, studying its dark surface. Up close the stone took on colour, the overall blackness fragmenting into shades that seemed to combine to cloak the mesa in darkness. Green striated the surface where water ran from the flat top, sixty or seventy feet above the surrounding terrain. Ochre and a dull red spread with gold and a dark bluish taint. Where the sun hit, the rock seemed to contain massive veins of gold, or shone like polished coal. Wrinkles corrugated the vertical walls, water moistening the stone on the shadowed side, burned off sunwards. There were no cracks or splits deep enough to hide a man, nor were the walls climbable.

Jennings halted in the shadow and swung an elbow round into the woman's ribs. Rosita shrieked as she was toppled from the buckskin pony, landing on the sand in a flurry of petticoats and flailing legs. She rolled over, tugging her skirts down as she climbed to ther feet. The green dress hung open at the front, the buttons burst when Jennings seized her, the silk stained dark with dried blood. Beneath, her camisole was dirty, stained by trail dust and sweat and the blood that had dripped from her mouth and nose. Her hair was tangled, fallen from its neat pinnings to tumble wild about her face. That was marked by Jennings' blows. Both cheeks were purpled with bruises, the mottling running into the blue-yellow discoloration encircling one swollen eye. Her lips were puffed up, cuts dark against the bruised pink, the lower thrust out over the swelling where a tooth had broken. She stared at Jennings with a gaze that combined hate and resignation.

The tall man ignored her as he swung clear of the saddle.

'This'll do it.' He looked around, calculating the dimensions of the rock. 'You send the message in soon as it's light, Simon. I figger Wyatt'll come runnin' soon as he gets it. That means the shadow'll be on the west side, so I'll be there. Waiting.'

'Suppose he don't come?' Coltrane didn't believe it. 'What then?'

'He comes out later. I'll move round with the shadow.' Jennings' smile was confident. 'I got the spy glass, an' I'll see yore dust. You make goddam sure you pick a good spot.'

Coltrane nodded, then: 'Suppose he ain't alone?'

'He will be.' Jennings went on smiling, his dark eyes fierce. 'The message'll make sure of that.'

'Maybe he won't come at all.' Coltrane voiced a final hope. 'What do we do if he just don't come at all?'

'You think he'll let us cut the woman?' Jennings looked at Rosita for the first time, and she shuddered. 'He ain't that kind o' man.'

He shook his head, certain of himself. Certain that Wyatt was going to do exactly as he had it planned.

'All right,' he said, the smile fading. 'We'll rest up here tonight. Afore it gets light, you two ride out an' get in position. Come dawn you send the horse in. Then we wait for Wyatt to show.'

Coltrane nodded again and began to unsaddle his pony.

'I hope it ain't injuns.' Abner Teech curled his hands around his glass like a man trying to squeeze confidence out of the whiskey. 'I hope that renegade ain't hit the stage.'

'Or outlaws.' Doc Mortimer glanced at Wyatt as he said it. 'Maybe Jennings.'

Wyatt drank, staring at the picture Mortimer had hung on the wall. It looked to have been painted in a place a whole lot different to Black Rock. There was a stream running through a wood heavy with leaves. Blue sky showed through the branches, streaked with white cloud. There was a deer of some kind he didn't recognize looking over the water to where a blonde girl in a white robe was reaching for an equally fair man in some kind of funny-looking blue outfit. Cole Garrett had used to have a portrait of his wife hung there.

'I changed things around.' Doc Mortimer followed

Wyatt's gaze. 'Didn't seem right having Cole's things. Not the personal stuff. So I packed them over to your cabin.'

Wyatt nodded absently, grey eyes suddenly cloudy with thought.

'It's not too likely to be hostiles,' he said. 'The Army's got patrols out, an' they figure Salvaje went over the border. Anyway, he's got around a hundred bucks with him; they'll need feeding. He's more likely to hit a ranch than risk bringing a patrol down because a stage don't turn up on schedule.'

'We ain't seen Army.' Teech sniffed noisily and helped himself to more whiskey. 'First we heard about hostiles was from you.'

'Maybe they stayed over someplace.' As he said it, Wyatt realised it was more question than statement. 'Waiting for word.'

'From who?' Teech asked.

'The Army?' Wyatt shrugged, wondering why he was feeling doubt. 'An escort? Or maybe just word that the road was clear.'

'Ben Savanker was driving that run.' Teech's head moved slowly from side to side, his voice negative. 'He wouldn't wait up three days for an escort.'

Wyatt nodded again, mouth tightening. When he didn't speak, Doc Mortimer said:

'They'd maybe take the same trail as the stage.'

He didn't need to say who the *they* were.

'Be faster overland.' Wyatt frowned. 'Stage road allows for loaded coaches. Man on a horse moves faster.'

'So why aren't they here?' Mortimer rose to his feet, staggering slightly as he crossed the room to fetch a second bottle from the glass-fronted cabinet. 'It's three days now since you rode in.'

'Depends when they got to Terlingua.' Wyatt shrugged, the frown still on his face. 'I don't know how long they waited at the Tres Pinos crossing. Could be they ran into Salvaje's bunch. Tyson couldn't get word to them, not before they reached Terlingua. Why'd Jennings do it, anyway?'

As he said it, the doubts clarified, taking shape in a form that sent cold anger raging through him as he recognized the fear. His feelings had died with Josie. Hate and rage and pain had filled him, coalescing in the core of ruthless anger that pushed him on, prompted him to make the metal hand, to kill. Just as Doc had said, he was turned killer. He had lived – did live – to see his wife's murderers die. There was no other purpose, and therefore no other concern. There was no room for concern. And yet he felt it now: for Rosita Vasquez. For a goddam Mexican singer most likely heading for an Albuquerque whorehouse. If Jennings hadn't got to her first. And that brought the cold anger flooding up to suppress the fear. There was no reason he should give a damn what happened to the woman. She meant nothing to him. Hell! She'd offered herself and he just hadn't wanted her. Hadn't even been tempted: it was too close after Josie. He felt the anger turn inwards. It felt like a kind of betrayal of Josie.

'The woman.' Mortimer's whiskey-slurred voice cut hard to the centre of Wyatt's thoughts, putting them into words he didn't want to hear. 'You said you brought her up from the border after her boyfriend got the silver route changed. Then you stopped over in Terlingua – people saw you together. It makes sense, Tyler. Maybe Jennings got word you were together, so he went after the stage.'

'Why?' The big man said it hoping to hear an answer that would clear his doubts. 'He'd know I was waiting for him here. He'd come after me. Maybe try to catch me on the trail. Why go after Rosita?'

Mortimer topped his glass and swallowed half before he spoke again. When he did, Wyatt's doubts weren't cleared.

'Revenge? He must be crazy. To do what he did here. Maybe he'd want to take her because she was with you. Maybe he heard about her boyfriend.'

Wyatt swallowed whiskey. Mortimer's words triggered

off a remembrance of Josie. Down on the floor with her dress ripping from her body. He blanked it off, refusing to see the rest.

'Maybe.' His voice was cold. 'But they'll still come here.'

'I guess.' Mortimer stared at thc younger man. 'And you'll be waiting.'

'Yeah.' Wyatt smiled. 'I'll be waiting.'

'Alone,' the doctor said.

'Yeah.' Wyatt looked at the metal where his left arm ended. 'Singlehanded.'

Chapter Twelve

TYLER WYATT. I GOT ROSITA VASKEZZ. OUT BIE THE MAYSA. YOU COME OUT ALONE OR I CUT HER UP LIKE I CUT YOR FREND COLE GARRETT. COME NOW. DOENT BRING NO ONE WITH YOU OR YOU GET HER BACK IN BITS. VANCE JENNINGS.

The note was lettered in stark capitals, Jennings' signature scrawled beneath the printed name. Simon Coltrane read it through with his lips moving and passed it back to Jennings.

'Guess that says it.'

'Yeah.' Jennings nodded, pleased with himself. 'That'll bring him out. An' this.'

He reached to the side, winding his hand in the woman's hair. Rosita screamed as she was yanked sideways, feet waving dangerously close to the fire. She heard the scrape of the outlaw's sabre lifting from the sheath and closed her eyes on the raw knot of panic chilling her belly as she waited for the edge to touch her throat.

'Not yet, lady.' Jennings husked laughter as he hacked a strand of hair loose. 'This is just to let the blacksmith know fer sure we got you.'

He knotted the hair and passed it to Coltrane.

'Send him that, too.'

The fair-haired man grunted, reaching for the note. He folded it and then tied the hair around the rectangle of greasy paper.

'That should do it.' He pushed the note into his tunic.

'Yeah. Now get going.' Jennings sheathed the sabre. 'An' do it right.'

Coltrane ducked his head and climbed to his feet. Jennings watched as he put his saddle on the piebald and waited for Cannon to saddle the other two animals. They mounted up, firelight transforming the scar-faced man's ugly smile to an expression of pure evil. Coltrane looked sorry for himself. Cannon took the reins of Jennings' buckskin in his left hand and took the pony out behind him. Coltrane followed, slumped in the saddle.

'Just you an' me.' Jennings turned his face towards the woman. All alone.'

Rosita tugged her torn dress across her bosom, eyes wary as the outlaw smiled.

'Don't worry.' His whisper rustled through the crackle of burning wood. 'I ain't gonna touch you. Not yet. You better worry about Wyatt showin'. He don't, you're gonna lose an ear.'

Tears filled the woman's eyes as he stroked the hilt of the sabre, still fixing her with that death's head smile.

Light showed where Black Rock stood, twinkling through the darkness closer than Coltrane liked. Above, the moon was filled out, not yet a full circle, but still rounded enough it lit the flatlands with a pale, ghostly light. The fair-haired man pointed at a stretch of sand shining white against the surrounding cholla and said, 'There. That's good as any other.'

Strother Cannon nodded and began to use the stock of his Winchester to scoop out a hollow. Coltrane joined him, scraping out sufficient sand that a shallow indentation remained. He took a blanket from his saddle and spread it over the hollow, spreading more sand over the rough woollen surface. He'd most likely lose some when he got bellied down underneath, but the blanket was a tan colour anyway, and the cholla would blend it in. He turned so his mouth was facing Cannon, as though the scarred man's muteness also meant deafness.

'You come up goddam fast when you hear me fire, Strother. I ain't takin' no chances.'

Cannon nodded, his teeth leprous in the moonlight. He swung round, climbing onto his roan gelding to shade into the darkness down the trail.

Coltrane listened to the hoofbeats fade, calculating the distance the mute would need to cover. Calculating times. It seemed like too goddam far and too goddam long, but there wasn't anything he could do about it now. Except keep on hoping it came off like Vance wanted. That, and wait.

He went over to the piebald and fastened the note to the saddlehorn with the woman's hair. He made sure it was tied on tight enough it wouldn't blow loose, then he scooped up a handful of dried-out chaparral and knotted it inside his bandanna. He left enough of the twigs jutting out that the tinder would take fire, then hiked up the piebald's tail and fastened the bundle close to its rump. The horse snickered, irritated by the handling, and Coltrane murmured to it, gentling it. That done, he checked over his Winchester, levering the shells out and brushing each one carefully clean before thumbing it back through the loading gate. He got down on his belly beside the hollow, sighting the carbine at the trail as he calculated angles.

The spot he had chosen stretched down from a slight curve in the trail from Black Rock. Cholla grew around two sides of the sand, putting bulk between him and the trail so he'd be out of sight until Wyatt rounded the curve. That was marked by a single saguarro that jutted up against the night sky like a pointer. Wyatt would come around that onto the straight stretch flanked by the sand. Straight on to Coltrane's gun. If Coltrane could shift the blanket fast enough, he should be able to get in one shot before Wyatt even saw him. The blacksmith would most likely be riding hard, so the falling horse should pitch him over its head and maybe that would lay him out. At least it should give Coltrane time to get a fresh shell in the breech so Wyatt would be covered.

If he was running.

If he wasn't, then it was going to be harder. Not impossible, but considerably more risky.

If Wyatt came up slow, it would be harder to hear the hoofbeats, so calculating the time to show would be more difficult. And if he was riding slow, then he could have time to clear the horse. Coltrane got up off the sand and walked to where the saguarro marked the curve. Peering into the moonlit darkness he tried to imagine the scene from horseback. The saguarro would be on the rider's right and that could pull his eye over so he'd be looking away from Coltrane's position. Then the cholla would hide a lot of the sand, so if Wyatt was getting up from a fall – shaken up, maybe, too – he wouldn't know exactly where the shot had come from. Coltrane could have the Winchester reloaded before the blacksmith saw him. And Wyatt would lose his rifle, if he carried one, on the downed horse. He'd be using a handgun, if he had the time to use anything at all, and that wouldn't be too accurate over the distance. Coltrane could put a shot past him if necessary. Just to let him know he didn't have a chance and he'd better drop his gun.

If he didn't, then it would have to be a wounding. Which Coltrane didn't think about as he paced back to the waiting horse. He took a three quarters full bottle from the saddlebag and hunkered down on the cold sand with the whiskey to warm him. He didn't feel much like sleeping.

The night got colder, dew frosting the cactus with moisture that shone in the moon's light. Then the sky blurred, the stars fading as the moon shifted over to the west. The transient brightness of the false dawn shaded the prairie a misty gold, and Coltrane swallowed the last of his whiskey and tossed the bottle away into the brush. He watched the light fade again, the morning blacker than the night. Then saw shafts of brilliant gold thrust through the darkness as the sun came up over the eastern skyline. Like a curtain drawn back across the heavens, the night receded. Gold spread steadily from the east, fading as it covered an increasingly wider area to give way to blue.

Coltrane took the piebald up to the curve in the trail. The hard packed sand ran straight in from there. Straight in to Black Rock. Nothing to stop the pony and too much cholla along the way for it to veer off.

He drew the reins back, looping them around the saddlehorn, around the note. Then he eased back along the animal's side, stroking it and murmuring to it as he pulled a match from his tunic and struck it on his holster. The piebald's head started to turn as the phosphor flared into life, but before it knew what was happening, Coltrane had the match thrust in under its tail.

Hair singed as the tinder flamed. The pony lashed its tail, bucking high so that the bundle was waved through the air, its passage speeding the spread of the flames. Inside the bandanna, the timber smouldered into life. Heat burst pain against the horse's tender rump. It smelled hair burning as the flames began to consume the kerchief and its tail took fire.

It screamed and thundered away in the direction of the settlement.

Coltrane ran back to the sand. He grabbed his Winchester and wriggled partway under the blanket. Then he began to scoop sand over the cloth; furiously. He covered as much as he could and got down flat in the hollow, reaching out to palm back more sand, working blind. He eased the corners of the blanket over two rocks, so that a two-inch gap remained between sand and cloth, the muzzle of the carbine pointing out at the trail.

He eased himself comfortable and pressed the Winchester against his shoulder. By day's light it didn't look too different: his calculations should work out right.

He settled down to wait, trying to ignore the heat that

burned against his back and sent sweat trickling salty over his face. The whiskey had dried him, and he couldn't resist the temptation to swig from the canteen set beside the Winchester. It was like a furnace under the blanket.

And the thought made him grin tightly. Wyatt had been a blacksmith: he used a furnace. And now Vance was going to send him to a different kind of heat.

'You're goin' to hell,' Coltrane muttered. Then shook his head, chuckling. 'No you ain't. You're comin' to hell. An' when I get the woman, so'll I.'

He chuckled quite a lot as he waited.

Chapter Thirteen

Wilbur Meacham's brindle hound saw the runaway pony first and set to barking loud enough its owner came out to see what the hell was getting at the dog. He saw the piebald horse charging riderless into Black Rock and ran into the centre of the street yelling and waving his arms. The horse saw him and veered away, so the dog went after it, nipping close enough at its heels that the animal slowed right down and began to buck. Willy Honniger heard the horse screaming and the dog yapping and Wilbur Meacham yelling and came out of his grain store with lather from his morning shave still on his face.

Tyler Wyatt came out from the Belle fully dressed with a Colt in his right hand. He saw Meacham and Honniger grabbing at the horse and Truett Pailey slapping at its tail. Abner Teech slung a bucket of water at the haunches and the pony gentled down.

'That's an Apache trick.' Abner Teech stared over the prairie as he said it. 'Puttin' fire under the tail.'

'There's a note.' Wilbur Meacham pointed at the saddlehorn. 'Got yore name on it, Tyler.'

Wyatt stepped closer as Meacham unwound the reins. There was a rectangle of greasy paper tied to the saddlehorn with what looked like hair. Raven black hair. Black as Josie's had been blonde. He recognized it. Eyes cold, he slid one metal blade under the hair, slicing it. The name on the paper, set in big capital letters, was *Tyler Wyatt*.

He opened the paper, scanning the words written there, then folded it. His face was tense, a cold, threatening anger blazing in his eyes as he climbed up on the sidewalk, staring at the men grouped around the horse, the women watching from windows and verandahs.

'This ain't nothing to do with you!' His voice was a cold whiplash of command, menacing as his eyes. 'This is between me and them. No one else.'

Truett Pailey said, 'Jesus, Tyler! You mean the Jennings bunch.'

Willy Honniger said, 'You can't go against them alone, Tyler. What's the note say?'

'No.' Wyatt shook his head. 'They're mine! No one comes with me.'

'You ain't gonna stop us,' said Pailey. 'We're backin' you.'

Wyatt looked at him and Pailey closed his mouth. No one doubted him when he said, 'I'll kill anyone tries to follow me.'

They watched him turn away, going back inside the Belle, and then stared at one another, not wanting to say the words in all their minds: *Tyler Wyatt's turned killer*.

As Wyatt paced down the saloon, Doc Mortimer came out from the door at the end. Shirt tails fluttered over drooping braces, and he hopped on one foot, fumbling with a lace-up boot. His eyes were whiskey-reddened, but alert, his crumpled face frowning.

'What is it?' He tugged the laces into place as Wyatt went past him into the room. 'What's happened?'

Wyatt passed him the note and began to check the loads in his Colt. Mortimer sat down at the table, smoothing the paper flat.

'My God!' His voice was hushed and hoarse. 'That must be why the stage is late.'

'Yeah.' Wyatt lifted his Winchester. 'Jennings wants to draw me out. This is his way.'

'You can circle round.' Mortimer stood up as Wyatt headed for the door. 'He's waiting at Black Rock, you can go around. Come up on him from behind.'

'No.' Wyatt shook his head as he made for the batwings, Mortimer hurrying after him. 'They sent a horse in. That means at least one of them came in close. He's either waitin' for me or on his way back to the mesa. I figure to catch him.'

Mortimer squinted in the sunlight as they went down the sidewalk. 'He's waiting, you'll be riding into an ambuscade.'

'I don't think so.' They reached the livery and Wyatt went down to the stall holding the bay stallion. 'Jennings wants me out alone.'

'So he doesn't want to risk a shoot-out with a posse.' Mortimer watched as the big man with the metal hand slung the saddle over the bay. 'He just wants you.'

'Like I want him,' Wyatt said, cinching the saddle tight. 'That's why he took Rosita – to guarantee I'll do like he says. He wants me alive. The same way he wanted Cole.'

'And you're still going out?' Mortimer saw the Winchester drop into the saddle scabbard. 'Alone? Straight?'

'Sure.' Wyatt brought the bay out of the stall. Began to lead it down towards the doors. 'If there is an ambush an' Jennings wants me alive, they'll aim for the horse. And I know the country, Doc. Josie an' me used to ride out that way a lot.'

His face clamped tight on the last words and he swung onto the saddle with cold fire in his grey eyes. Sun's light glinted bright off the metal hand, the quality of the reflection changing where it came off the freshly-honed edges of the three blades jutting like claws from the fist.

Mortimer said, 'Be careful.' And it sounded like, 'Goodbye.'

'I told them not to follow me.' Wyatt held the stallion in check as the animal sensed his impatience, his fury. 'I told them I'd kill anyone tried it. Don't let that happen.'

'No.' Mortimer shook his head as Wyatt let the bay horse out. 'I'll try.'

* * *

No one tried to stop Wyatt as he thundered down Main Street. No one ran for horse or gun. Instead they just stood there, watching him ride out and remembering the way his eyes had looked.

Doc Mortimer didn't need to warn anyone. There was no one about to chance going up against Tyler Wyatt.

Tyler Wyatt's turned killer.

Wyatt got outside of town and eased the bay down to a fast canter. Up ahead, he could see the stark outline of the mesa, the sun not yet high enough to swathe it in heat haze. The trail to the rock stretched before him, straight save for a few long curves where wagons had skirted stands of mesquite. It was mostly like that: a ribbon of yellow running through the heavy chaparral and the globes of cholla, the view ahead clear for long stretches. Except where the sharper curves swung round hard enough that forwards sight was blocked.

That would be the place: one of the curves.

If there was an ambush.

He slowed some more, not letting his pace slacken enough a hidden watcher might guess he was wary, but sufficient that he could scan the terrain ahead. There was chaparral growing in too close and too thick anyone could wriggle under it, and the mesquite was too far out to guarantee a bullet in the horse.

If that was Jennings' plan.

The fury told him that was how he had to read it. Anything else had to dictate caution – that he circle round like Doc had suggested. But then Jennings might start cutting the woman. He wasn't sure whether the fear he felt was for Rosita or for the responsibility of another woman's life. And the doubt stoked the rage, focussing into cold determination that brought his senses to a peak of lethal anticipation.

There was no dust on the trail ahead. No plume to show a horse running back for the mesa.

So it had to be an ambush.

There had to be someone waiting for him between his present position and Black Rock.

He wondered which it was.

Simon Coltrane waved a fly from his face and brushed sweat from his eyes. He wanted to take a leak. His belly was chilled from the night-cold sand and his back was burning as the sun got higher. His mouth felt like the inside of a tobacco pouch, but he didn't want to chance drinking any more water. He eased his hips around, trying to take pressure off his swollen bladder. It did no good – mostly just reminded him how uncomfortable he felt.

Then he heard a dull, faint drumming in the sand.

He pressed his ear to the ground. Yeah! That was hoofs. And coming at speed, too. Getting closer fast.

He lifted his head, settling the stock of the Winchester against his shoulder. The hammer clicked loud in the heat-filled stillness under the blanket as he curled his forefinger around the trigger, sighting down the muzzle to place the upright fin of the foresight between the open legs of the vee-shaped rear-sight. He allowed for the angle, estimating the trajectory between his position and the chest of a horse as it rounded the curve beside the big saguarro.

The drumming in the sand got more insistant. Louder. Grains trembled and began to run in streamers down the edges of the hollow. Coltrane breathed in deep, letting it out slow as his finger tightened on the trigger and a bay horse came round the curve.

A curve. It had to be. That was the only place a man could hide. Stay out of sight until a rider was on him. But if Jennings wanted him alive, then the shootist had to try for the horse. So he'd need time to make a clear shot. And that had to mean a straight length on the far side of the curve. Somewhere a man's line of fire wouldn't be obstructed by the undergrowth. Like a patch of sand. Clear of cactus and stretched alongside the trail.

Only then Wyatt would spot him as he rounded the curve. Because the sand had to be bare to allow for the shot.

And the big man smiled as he remembered the Apaches.

That could be it: a shootist dug into the sand with a blanket over him. Just a Winchester muzzle pointed out, lined on the trail.

He saw a lone saguarro rising ahead, and his memory told him there was a stretch of open ground beyond it. After the curve. He slowed the horse slightly, eyes moving from side to side. Looking for warning of some kind.

Something glinted amongst the chaparral to his left. It was beyond the curve, past the saguarro and on the opposite side of the ribbon of sand. It caught the sun like glass, shining amongst the duller underbrush. Wyatt took the bay wide around the saguarro, tensing in the saddle.

There was a movement ahead. It was too small and too sudden to register clearly on his vision: he had no exact image. But it was sufficient warning that he was lifting from the saddle as muzzle flash sparked and the blast of a carbine rolled over the sand.

The bay stallion went down with a red hole spouting blood from its chest. It hit dirt and somersaulted, ruptured heart pumping dark crimson from the wound. Wyatt came off with his legs pumping, seeking balance as he used the momentum of the downed horse to propel him forwards in a crazy, arm-flailing run towards the man lifting from the sand.

He saw a faded cavalry tunic. Simon Coltrane's slack face, twisting now in what was either a shout of fear or a yell of triumph. Saw the Winchester's lever snap shut, the ejected shell glittering as it arced through the air. Saw the carbine lift as Coltrane came up on his knees. And he hurled himself down in a wild dive that carried him under the bullet, his left shoulder hitting sand, taking the impact as he rolled, twisting to his feet with his legs still working to power him forwards.

Coltrane was levering the Winchester, eyes widening as he saw Wyatt still coming at him. The big man had his arms thrust out like he was reaching for Coltrane, his lips curled back in a feral snarl. The metal hand flashed bright, light blurring Coltrane's vision as hands wet with fear-sweat slithered on the carbine.

Wyatt hit the man at a run. His left arm swung round, the blades smashing against the Winchester, tearing it from Coltrane's grip. His shoulder struck the fair-haired man in the chest, hurling him back, his boots losing footing in the hollow so that he crashed down with Wyatt on top. The big man brought his arm back. Coltrane screamed as he tried to reach the Colt holstered on his waist and felt a blow jerk his hand clear of the pistol.

Wyatt pulled his arm back and Coltrane's scream pitched higher as the blades tore loose from flesh. They went back with blood sliming the steel, thin spurts of scarlet marking where they had torn the bicep. Wyatt rolled clear, lurching to his knees. Coltrane scrabbled backwards, his arm dragging by his side, flapping loose where the muscles and the tendons were cut. He left a trail behind him, flies settling on the warm blood in oblivious feasting. He reached his left arm across his belly, unaware that his bladder was emptying its load in a spreading, acrid stain across his pants as he stretched his fingers towards the Colt.

The metal hand lifted again. It slashed down and forwards as Wyatt stretched towards Coltrane. The blades hacked over the left arm, scoring lines that were abruptly edged with crimson through the faded blue of the cavalry tunic. Through the pale flesh of Coltrane's upper arm. It swung again, the points landing now, piercing cloth and flesh, cutting deep into the muscle of the upper arm.

Wyatt twisted the blades, gouging them free so that a great wash of crimson drenched the sleeve, splashing onto Coltrane's face. He pushed away from the screaming man, coming up on his feet. Hatred corded the tendons of his neck, drew out his features in a mask of pure rage.

'Stand up!' The voice was ugly as the face. Coltrane saw death shine cold in the grey eyes. 'Get on your feet.'

Coltrane stumbled upright as though hypnotized. Tears watered his vacant eyes as they stared into the savage features of the big man with the metal hand. His mouth hung slack as his useless hands, spittle frothing on the lower lip. He tried to say something. He wasn't sure what and it came out as a wailing shriek anyway as he saw the dripping blades move towards him again.

'For Cole Garrett.'

Fire scorched over Coltrane's belly. Blood soaked his tunic, oozing down to join the pungent stain covering the front of his pants. He shook his head, staggering backwards.

'For Josie.'

The blades slammed against Coltrane's jaw. They cut skin, grating over bone and gums as three gaping slashes lipped wide across the cheek. They came loose, droplets of crimson trailing behind. Coltrane's lips were severed, flapping in pieces from one side of his mouth. The left side was a red maw, the cheek opened from jaw to lips, the flesh hanging like fresh-butchered steak. Teeth showed, darkening as the slashed gums poured out blood. It coursed from the face, curtaining the lower jaw, running hot down the neck. It bubbled in the mouth, spilling over the teeth to wash down thick over the chin.

Wyatt smiled, moving steadily forwards as Coltrane backed away. The fair-haired man was shaking his head as though he tried to deny the pain. Deny his own dying. The movement sent blood spraying over his shoulders, flapping the chunks of loose flesh dangling from his face. It flooded from the wounds, masking the lower part of his head like a scarlet bandanna. His arms waved at his sides, useless below the elbows, crimson still pulsing from the cuts so that his sleeves were dark, as though plunged into water. His hands were slick, painted red, the stuff dripping from his fingers. More came from his belly, spurting as his retreating steps pressed organs tighter against the open slashes.

Wyatt paused as Coltrane reached the chaparral. He stood waiting as the blood-soaked man tottered, then regained his balance, staring wildly round as he realized the brush had ended his retreat. Tears welled from his eyes, mingling with the streamers of mucus trailing from his nose, the crimson masking his jaw.

'You're dying.' Wyatt's voice was harsh, rasping from between teeth clenched in a deathmask smile. 'Like Cole did. Like Josie.'

'No.' The single word was thick, moaning through the blood, distorted by the opened face. The next was lost, but it was the same: 'No.'

Wyatt ignored it as he said, 'For me.'

And drove the metal hand up in a curving arc that ended where Coltrane's underjaw joined his neck.

The blades ripped through the soft flesh, driving up through the floor of the mouth into the tongue, then continued their upwards movement, driven on by all the force in Wyatt's muscular body. They pierced the roof of the mouth, tearing into the sinus cavities to send thick columns of scarlet jetting from Coltrane's nostrils. They touched the brain, and Coltrane jerked, spasms wracking his body. His heels lifted, toes clearing the ground as Wyatt's blow raised him, the weight of his own body adding to the ruin of his skull, dragging him down harder as the blades drove upwards. An eye popped from its socket, bouncing bloody against the open cheek. Crimson welled from the staring hole.

Wyatt stood, muscles bulging across his shoulders, feet braced wide, right hand fastened about the metal of his left arm as he held Coltrane off the ground. Blood ran thick down his forearms, soaking into his shirt-sleeves. More splashed over his face. He ignored it, his eyes fastened on the man twitching on the hooks of his hand.

Coltrane's body went on trembling as the life died in his remaining eye. His bowels opened, the stink of excrement momentarily overpowering the sweetish odour of the blood, the sickly wafting coming from the ripped belly. His head jerked in wild circles, teeth clattering together as the spasms reached a crescendo that stretched his head back, as though he sought to drag himself loose from the blades. Then his mouth snapped shut and the head lolled, pieces of flesh dangling close to Wyatt's eyes.

The big man dropped his arm, letting the corpse fall to the sand. He tugged the metal hand clear, staring at the bloody tines, the smile still on his face.

And then a sound intruded on his mind.

The killing fury that had gripped him had focussed all his attention on Coltrane. He had been obsessed with the man's dying, seeing only the wounds opening on the body, hearing only the sound of Coltrane's voice. His lust for vengeance had blocked out any other sights. Any other sounds.

Like hoofbeats.

Wyatt swung round as Strother Cannon came charging onto the sand. The big, scar-faced man was up on a roan with a buckskin pony thundering close behind. His mouth was stretched back in a wordless yell, the scars decorating his features showing white and dead against the brown of his skin. He was driving the roan straight at Wyatt.

The big man swung his metal hand at the roan's nose in a useless attempt to turn the charge. It was too late. The animal hit him at full gallop. It smashed him off his feet, hurling him back into the brush. Then its legs tangled in the chaparral and it went down after the man. Strother Cannon was tossed from the saddle, flying out over the tangled undergrowth with his bellow turning to a shout of surprise.

He felt thorns stab his body, tearing like talons. And the pain made him think of claws. Like the ones the Mexican woman said Wyatt wore. He struggled against the thorns, their sharpness crazing him as he remembered what Rafe Coombes had looked like. What the Mexican woman had said they called Wyatt: *El Garra*.

He didn't want to feel those claws.

Chapter Fourteen

Wyatt felt no pain.

There was only impact, smashing him backwards with the breath gusting from his lungs so fast he was unaware of the chaparral that cushioned his fall. The fury filled him, numbing him to the sharp grip of the tangled plants as he surged to his feet. His back was speckled with blood and more oozed from a torn cheek as he shook his head, fighting to clear his blurred vision.

There was a dull ringing inside his head that made the brush surge and shimmer, seeming to come at him in waves that were multicoloured as the lights dancing over his eyes. It was more instinct than certainty that propelled him forwards, lumbering through the chaparral towards Strother Cannon.

The scarred man was bellowing like a gelded bullock as he fought the grip of the vegetation. Blood painted the scars where he had gone face-down into the chaparral, crimson spilling over his arms and chest as he struggled. Wyatt felt the brush tug at his pants, slowing him. Cholla thrust painful needles into his legs: he didn't feel them. He was intent only on reaching Cannon before the killer got loose and drew the LeMat. He'd use it now, the way his face looked. It was crazy enough he'd forget any plans that Jennings might have and just do what he did best: kill.

Wyatt felt fear knot cold inside him. Not fear of death. Not fear for the woman. It was the fear that he might die too early. Before he could kill Cannon. Go on after Jennings.

The fear drove him through the chaparral in a wild run that would have been impossible had he not been gripped by a kind of madness. The cactus that ripped his legs went unnoticed. His vision cleared, shock driven off by the fury and the fear. He saw Cannon struggle to his feet. Flailed his arms as a root snagged his heel and threatened to pitch him down. Saw the bloodied face turn towards him. Kicked through groping branches. Saw the big hand close on the rounded grip of the LeMat.

Strother Cannon felt his hand circle the familiar butt. He raised his left arm, smearing blood across his face as he wiped it clear of his eyes. The massive shotgun-pistol slid from the holster with practised ease. Cannon thumbed the hammer back, the cylinder rolling a loaded chamber under the firing pin. He began to raise the gun, arm thrust out straight, blood all over it, to where Wyatt was coming through the chaparral.

He squeezed the trigger, the LeMat bucking in his hand as the .42 slug blasted from the muzzle. Powder smoke filled the air, obscuring his sight for a moment as he cocked the pistol again.

It was a moment too long: Wyatt came through the smoke with a smile on his face like the angel of death and the metal hand reaching out for Cannon's life.

Wyatt saw the pistol lifting as he closed the distance. Pure instinct lifted his left arm in a defensive gesture that set the metal hand out towards the flaming muzzle. The slug hit the hand, blasting nervous shock up his arm as it ricochetted off the metal. Again, there was no sensation of pain, only a numbness that seemed to freeze his shoulder, locking his arm in place as he hurled himself at Cannon.

The scar-faced man was turning, putting his body sideways on to Wyatt's charge with the instinctive movement of an experienced shootist. Wyatt's shoulder landed under the arm, his own locked forwards before his face. He heard the roar of the LeMat as it detonated a second time, close to his head. Felt the searing blast of the flame scorch his neck. Cannon's face was close enough he caught the sour breath gusting from the twisted mouth, stared directly into wild eyes with madness fighting recognition inside the orbs.

Then he saw the blades cut through the yellow material of Cannon's shirt as the impact drove them together. Blood welled around the tines, spreading over cotton so that each patch joined in a single, widening blot. The LeMat blasted again, and the scar-faced man's left hand came over to grab at Wyatt's wrist. The brown-haired man clamped his own good hand on Cannon's forearm. His fingers dug deep into the flesh as he fought to hold back the scalped man's grasp. Tendons stood out from both men's arms. Their strength was equal and the threat of death was equal.

The metal hand was gouging deeper into Cannon's throat. The blades had landed where the breastbone dipped, only thin skin protecting the windpipe beneath. Wind was whistling from the holes, blood bubbling in the scarred man's mouth. His breath came in heaving gasps as he fought to suck air down into his starving lungs. But he still held the pistol, and he was bringing his right arm back, turning the heavy barrel of the LeMat towards Wyatt's head.

Wyatt twisted as he sensed the gun angled towards him. He tried to bend his left elbow, to swing closer against Cannon and let the bullet go past him. But his arm was still frozen by the paralysis of the ricochet. It remained stiff, so that the weight of his body dragged it round, tearing the metal hand out from Cannon's throat.

It came loose on a great spurt of crimson, gobbets of flesh clinging red and sticky to the tines. The lacerated skull bent back, a bubbling scream frothing past the taut-stretched lips. The blades swung on, slashing down Cannon's underarm to open lips of red like hungry mouths from bicep to wrist. Jets of scarlet burst bright from cut veins, and severed tendons sprung the hand open against the kick of the LeMat. Wyatt felt the shot reverberate against his skull. Felt the smoke fill his nostrils. He saw the huge pistol fly useless into the chaparral. And the scalped man's insane features as Cannon swung a bloody fist at his face.

He took the punch on the metal hand. Cannon's eyes rounded in shock as the blades pierced between his knuckles, grating between the intricate linkages of bone, slicing nerves and tendons like cut string. Wyatt twisted his arm, feeling movement return, the blades ripping loose in a cloud of scarlet. The fingers swung useless from the mangled remnants of the palm, blood flooding down Cannon's wrist. Both hands were gone now, but he lifted his arms, swinging them to encircle Wyatt's neck.

Wyatt turned inside the deadly embrace. He brought his left knee up, ramming it hard between Cannon's thighs. Agony erupted through the mute as his genitals crushed beneath the impact. Blood gouted from his mouth as he screamed, doubling over with his arms flying loose of Wyatt. As he went over, Wyatt twisted the metal hand, driving up so that the claws entered the belly. He went on twisting it, gouging a great red-rimmed hole as Cannon writhed, turning to the side as he went down. Wyatt tore the hand away, flipping the mute over onto his back. Blood fountained from the gaping hole as Cannon's tortured body bucked in agony. Entrails ballooned against the opening, briefly halting the spurting blood. Then they burst loose, spilling out in glistening streamers as the scar-faced man's own contortions spread the wound wider.

Wyatt looked round. There was no sign of Jennings. No rider moving up the trail. No gun pointed on his back. There was only the roan, screaming as it fought free of the brush. The buckskin standing nervous farther along.

He looked at Cannon.

The scalped man was still now. The blood leeching from

the gashes on his arm and throat and belly was gouting slower. His strength was concentrated on the simple act of breathing, crimson runnels pouring from the corners of his mouth. Scarlet bubbles glittered on his lips as his eyes dulled, glazing as the life suppurated from his body. Wyatt stood panting, watching as Cannon died. The anger burned fierce inside him, demanding satisfaction.

He waited until there was no more blood and the bubbles on Cannon's lips burst in the heat. He watched as flies landed on the corpse, clustering black over the glistening red of the opened throat, the gaping belly.

Then he turned away, staring to where the mesa jutted from the flatlands, dark as the sun moved farther across the sky. The yellow ribbon of the trail pointed there, like a beckoning finger urging him closer to the darkness.

'Only you and me now, Jennings.' The words came rasping from his mouth like curses. 'It didn't work.'

He was aware he spoke to himself as he moved towards the roan horse, welcoming the madness, welcoming the rage.

'You thought you had me hooked. Like a fish on a line.' He stared at the bloody tines of the metal hand, not knowing he smiled. 'Only the hook's in you. And I'm going to gut you.'

He climbed onto the saddle and urged the buckskin out from the chaparral, turning it down the trail. To where the black mesa waited.

To where Vance Jennings waited.